"I WAS WATCHING YOU when you met Andrew Brooke. I saw and heard everything."

Meade's heart began to thump.

The housekeeper's black eyes were vigilant. "That bothers you? Well, it ought to. Talk of divorce! All that money! And your husband died that very night of poison from a drink you mixed for him." She leaned forward. "What man wouldn't want some of that wealth? Maybe you two together planned Mr. Havlock's murder. A girl Andrew Brooke once wanted but then doesn't want until she is very rich. And if her husband doesn't want a divorce, then take the shortcut. Poison his drink. I expected you might have seen me watching you and Mr. Brooke, and perhaps you wanted to talk to me privately. Have you decided?"

"Decided?"

"Decided how much to pay me to keep quiet."

NINE O'CLOCK TIDE

Nine O'Clock Tide

MIGNON G. EBERHART

FAWCETT POPULAR LIBRARY • NEW YORK

NINE O'CLOCK TIDE

Published by Fawcett Popular Library, a unit of CBS Publications, the Consumer Publishing Division of CBS Inc., by arrangement with Random House, Inc.

ISBN: 0-445-04527-2

Printed in the United States of America

First Fawcett Popular Library printing: February 1980

10 9 8 7 6 5 4 3 2 1

One

"A good night for murder," said young Hoddy Forrest in as lugubrious a voice as he could summon. He dangled brown legs over the balustrade of the terrace and looked out at the still, evening waters of the Sound. Silence on the terrace behind him was disappointing; there was only Aunt Chrissy, sitting stiffly upright in a wicker chair nearby, her high-nosed face imperturbable as usual. Even the way her slim feet were planted together on the flagstone terrace suggested ice dignity. She didn't lift one of her carefully arched eyebrows but she had the ears of a cat, so she must have heard him but did not comment upon his ominous observation. He would have liked some sort of reaction to his deeply dramatic tones. He liked to think of himself in turn a poet *manqué* or an actor *manqué*. His sister, Meade, was likely to

5

say a little crisply that he was *manqué*, all right, and needn't brag about it. Meade was twenty-three; Hoddy was nineteen, going on twenty, and he had dramatic news for her. But Andy wouldn't wait very long; Hoddy swung his bare legs and dirty tennis shorts back over the balustrade and as he did so the door to the house opened; there was the clink of bottles and glasses and Meade emerged, laden with a tray of cocktail materials. Hoddy was not lacking in chivalry; he went to take the tray from her hands.

"Thanks," said Meade, who was, he reflected briefly, even to a brother whose sister's beauty had little importance, not without beauty. She had also during the past three years acquired poise and, he supposed, a degree of sophistication. All the same, the news he had for her would get through her outer skin of cool self-reliance; it was indeed a sensational situation. He put down the tray and she began at once to mix a drink for Sam. "How perfectly revolting," Hoddy said, diverted from his intended subject as he watched her assemble rye whiskey, maraschino cherries, two of them (Hoddy shivered), two tiny onions, a mint leaf, a dash of bitters. Her small tanned hands moved swiftly; she mixed her husband's drink every night for him, Hoddy knew; he watched fascinated while she held it up to the light, considered the color, said to herself, "I think that's just right," put the glass on the table and covered it with a paper napkin. She then looked up. "He adds what ice he wants."

Hoddy shook his head. "I don't see how Sam survives that!"

"It's what he likes. Now, Hoddy, you've really got to dress for dinner."

This wounded Hoddy. "But I *am* dressed!"

"In that awful old T-shirt and tennis shorts? I never saw such dirty tennis shoes in my life! The Garnets are coming to dinner." She rearranged

6

some glasses and looked in the ice bucket.

"Oh," Hoddy said thoughtfully. "Then I'll have to put off my talk with Sam till they've gone."

Meade's smooth brown head jerked up. "Oh, Hoddy! You *don't* want more money!"

He wiggled and looked from her steady blue eyes to the waters of the Sound.

But Meade was merciless. "Just last week you got back from three years in Paris. First you were going to learn to paint. Then you were going to write poetry. Sam paid every single bit of your expenses all that time. Now you *can't* ask him for more. I won't let you. Besides, if you'll just behave yourself, there may be a chance here. That is—of course you know that Brice was nominated for governor and has made a full circuit of the state. They haven't started on the heavy campaigning yet, but—" She shook his arm. "If Brice Garnet gets to be governor, he's sure to find some place for you. Please, Hoddy, be on your best behavior. *And go and clean up.*"

"Oh, all right. But—" He loved his sister, yet a glint of mischief came into his eyes. "I'll behave. I'll even dress." He looked down at himself plaintively. "Although I should have thought I looked all right for anybody. But I'll wash up and change if you'll do something for me."

Meade looked up warily; when his eyes were particularly candid and wide it was well to take care. "What?"

"It's what you will want, dearie." He let it out very dramatically. "Andy Brooke is waiting at the tennis court to see you."

Meade stepped back, striking the table so the glasses tinkled together. She was vaguely aware of Aunt Chrissy's suddenly fixed attention.

"Oh yes, he's here. Wants to see you. Waiting down there. I promised to send you down to see him."

7

Aunt Chrissy's pink linen dress rustled as she rose. "Meade, you've better sense than to go down there and see Andy!"

There were times when Aunt Chrissy's pronouncements riled Meade; this was one of them. "I don't see why not."

Aunt Chrissy didn't even blink. "You know perfectly well why not. You're a married woman. You are Mrs. Sam Havlock. You and Andy—"

"Go and see him, Meade," Hoddy broke in. "That's my advice. And it makes sense because he'll be hanging around Blue Water Cove for most of the summer. He says he's got to visit that cousin who brought him up. You can't avoid seeing him sometime. So you may as well get it over with, with no witnesses."

Of course, Aunt Chrissy was perfectly right. On the other hand, Meade argued swiftly to herself, it really might be easier to get through her first meeting with Andy with no keen-eyed observers who were too likely to remember too much.

Aunt Chrissy said, "Really, Meade! Don't be a stupid child."

This quite naturally fixed Meade in her own course. She did hold out a fraction of a moment longer, and Hoddy said, "Way you're acting now, anybody would think you still liked him. Why, anybody might wonder if maybe he jilted you and you married Sam on the rebound. And of course," Hoddy added philosophically, "that is exactly what you did. Can't fool me."

Perhaps she had fooled no one, Meade thought briefly; it didn't seem to matter now. But she must get Andrew Brooke off the place at once. Sam wouldn't want her to see Andy. There were things about Sam she wasn't sure about, but she was sure about that. She had to get rid of Andy; yet she would inevitably meet him sometime, somewhere, so it was better to do as Hoddy said, meet him for the first time alone.

Aunt Chrissy said sharply, "I forbid it. I absolutely forbid it!" which of course settled the question.

Hoddy helped. "Here." He had splashed some whiskey in a glass and a very little water on top of it. "Swallow this and hurry up. Can't have you fainting all over the place."

It stiffened her backbone. "I'm not the fainting type."

"Looked like it to me. White as a—well, now you're red. Give me that glass before you drop it. Go on down to the tennis court. And I'll dress properly enough to suit anybody, you'll see. Now go on."

Aunt Chrissy didn't quite hiss but might as well have done so in the sharp and disapproving breath she took. She then whisked into the house, obviously washing her delicate white hands of the whole affair.

Hoddy gave Meade an encouraging little push toward the flight of wrought-iron steps that led down to a small landing, where there was a bench. Here the steps divided: one short steep flight led down to the water; the other, longer one to the tennis court. Under the impetus of his brotherly shove and also Aunt Chrissy's opposition, which frequently aroused a sense of equal opposition in Meade, she descended the steps to the landing and then, suddenly, sat down on the bench; ought she to see Andy? Aunt Chrissy was often right. Better think, she told herself.

The quiet waters of the Sound, even the house above her took on a quality of waiting for something, a decision, an action, something. Yes, better think.

She had been married to Sam Havlock now for three years; she was still not at all certain of his reaction to anything. But surely he wouldn't want her, his wife, his possession, saying so much as a word to the man she had once been so in love with—even after Andy had jilted her, nicely, sensibly, but jilted her. Sam must have sensed this, although it was never easy to know just what Sam was thinking of or planning. Yes, it would be a mistake to see Andy at all.

The Havlock house itself was actually built on a small promontory which, on the east side of the house, sloped very abruptly down to the Sound. From the upper terrace, which rounded into a lovely oval with a wide balustrade around it (making, as Hoddy and everyone knew, for very pleasant sitting), stretched the long eastern view of the Sound. From this terrace to the Sound itself there were only boulders, scattered shrubbery, nothing artificial; certainly it had never been landscaped. There was only the short flight of steps, never used by the men who worked on the grounds.

But on the other side of the little promontory, pains had been taken; the whole had been filled in and leveled off well above the Sound; there were lawns and the tennis court, surrounded by fencing which was covered now with green vines. Overlooking the court, a second small terrace jutted out from the house, presumably to accommodate guests who wished to watch the tennis matches that had been in vogue in the days when the house was built; one could almost see ladies in long skirts, white shirtwaists and dashing sailor hats, advancing delicately to strike at a tennis ball and then possibly retire. Meade believed that Sam loved the place; after all, they had spent the last two summers here. But the architect and the Havlock who built the house had had romantic ideas as to beauty and grace, and almost no ideas at all about the conveniences of kitchens and bathrooms. These later additions Sam had permitted; otherwise the house remained almost a pleasant ghost of past times.

It had of course been built at a time when

"servant" was not an all but obsolete word; it was actually a three-story house, with a ground floor that was really a kind of cellar, once given over to servants, now mainly to storerooms; on the next floor were the living rooms, and on the third floor the bedrooms and baths. The bricks of the house had mellowed to a soft pinkish yellow; the stairs leading up past the ground floor to the massive mahogany front door were railed with intricately intertwined wrought iron, painted black. The front gates were of wrought iron too, so delicate that they looked lacy but were in fact very strong and usually bolted together at night unless forgotten. No one had ever, as far as Meade knew, ventured to approach the Havlock house on any nefarious errand.

Sam had unexpectedly solved the problem of domestic help for the summer; Florrie and John Elwell had been hired by Sam when, a summer theater having closed, they faced being out of work—"resting" was their word for it. As Sam explained it, since John had acted superbly as a butler, and Florrie with equal aplomb as a French maid, in the play in which he had seen them, he simply offered them a summer's job doing exactly what they did on the stage and brought them home in triumph. Mrs. Dunham came from somewhere too, every night, cooked a superb dinner, demanded an ultrasuperb price for her labor and drove away again in a new Mercedes-Benz. A crew of men calling themselves landscapers came once a week and kept the grounds tidy, clipped and trim. It was an age of specialization, said Sam.

So, in a rather odd but workable way, the house went on as gracefully as it had in a gracious era long past.

Now Andy was waiting for her on the tennis court. She hadn't seen him since the night, much like this, when he told her that he had no money and no job, and flatly asked her to break off their

11

engagement. After that she hadn't heard a word from him.

She had married Sam, rich, sophisticated Sam—a catch, Aunt Chrissy had said firmly—within three months. Even then she had known in her heart that it was all wrong; she couldn't marry anybody but Andy, who didn't want her. Aunt Chrissy had scolded her, finding her in tears on her wedding eve: "How lucky can you get!" Aunt Chrissy's words buttered no parsnips when she was really stirred. "Any girl in her senses would jump at the chance . . . good-looking, and all that Havlock money. Besides"—Aunt Chrissy drove the knife home—"Andy Brooke will never amount to anything. He hasn't got a dime. And in my opinion, never will have."

Meade had roused, although feebly, to deny this. "I don't care about Sam Havlock's money!"

"No?" said Aunt Chrissy. "But you'll soon get used to liking it."

And she did; she had to admit that to herself. Sam lavished gifts on her; clothes from famous dressmakers, furs and jewels—jewels that had to be kept in the bank most of the time, but he liked to get some out and decorate her with them when they were to attend some special social event or when he was invited to speak after dinner, as he so often was. In truth, in a very short time she began to accept the luxuries surrounding her. Gradually she built a kind of shell around herself, adjusted to the way of life Sam Havlock was giving her. She may have hardened a little in the process, and her growth may not have been the kind her father would have liked. "It's a very worldly way." She could almost hear her father say that. But her father's death was another of the reasons why she had married Sam. Andy didn't want her; her father had died. Hoddy was trying to find some kind of job, and failing, and Aunt Chrissy had poured forth all her powers of command, which

12

were great. So Meade, jilted, had soon married a man any girl would have wanted for a husband and whom probably many had tried to capture.

So there it was. The wise thing would be to turn around, climb the steps and try again to forget Andy.

The waters of the Sound were stealthily creeping in; the reedy undergrowth began to stir a little below all the crowding shrubbery. Actually, when the tide was at its full height, the waters almost touched the slightly mossy bricks of the ground floor. The water's near approach, according to Hoddy, could have afforded an excellent landing spot for smugglers: row up close to the house, smuggle freight into the ground-floor cellars, quickly and conveniently; then the smugglers could retire to their motorboats—no, Hoddy corrected himself, sailboats more likely until they were farther away—and there would be a cache of smuggled goods ready to make more money for the Havlocks. It was fascinating speculation—ironically, even to Meade—because all over the state now there were Havlock hospitals, Havlock schools for This and That, Havlock-built churches, Havlock bridges, Havlock highways. Sam himself had only followed family tradition. The fact was prosaic enough; with all the Havlocks now long gone except for Sam, the Havlock fortune which had been built slowly and carefully by wagon-manufacturing, investments in steel mills, investments in railroads, investments in anything that promised and produced rich returns, proclaimed a marked financial acumen in generations past.

Sam had let the arrangements made by his father many years ago continue in their way; the Havlock interests were controlled by a holding company; certain officers and directors of the holding company reported to Sam; his accountants, his lawyers, everyone in the Havlock organization was presumably under Sam's direct

13

guidance; actually, Meade believed, they guided his decisions and the Emmeline Holding Company prospered. Emmeline had been Sam's grandmother's name; it was the only touch of romanticism of which Meade had ever heard in the character of the Havlocks. The Emmeline Holding Company prospered, and Sam gave money, lavishly, almost anywhere.

The tide was advancing; she roused herself, rose and started down the steps to the tennis court. She knew she was in the wrong but her body simply refused to retreat; in fact nothing, nobody, could have induced her to turn back now that she saw Andy in the distance.

His figure, white shorts, white T-shirt, was outlined against the green mass of climbing vines which spread over the high fence in every direction. Andy was taking down the tennis net in an orderly fashion.

She was just as much in love with him as ever! It was as if she had been jolted awake from a three-year-old hypnotic kind of dream. It was as if she had suddenly, blindingly emerged from a false and bewildering night and come out into the reality of daylight.

Her own self-imposed arguments for grasping the nettle, so to speak, for seeing him now and getting over the inevitable meeting had no validity whatever. She had *had* to see him.

It was a physical shock; her body, her heart, her breath, every nerve seemed suddenly painfully alive, aware, racing. She didn't even think of turning and running back up all those steps. Instead she rushed toward him, and at that moment he turned, saw her, came swiftly to meet her, and she was tight in his arms.

She was pressed so close to him that she couldn't move and certainly did not want to move. It was a year, it was a century, it was a magic page out of

14

time before she began to murmur against his mouth, "No—no—no—"

"My dear, my darling." He held her closer.

"I've got to stop this—" It came out blurred, but he knew what she meant.

"What you've got to do is tell Sam. Get him to accept a divorce, in any way that suits him, so we can marry. I haven't got much, not a fortune like Sam, but now I've got a good job and enough to support you. But that doesn't seem to matter, because you belong to me and you know it."

"Sam..."

"You shouldn't have taken me so seriously when I said I couldn't marry you."

She drew back but still within the strong circle of his arms. "You *were* serious! You were very serious. You said you hoped it wouldn't hurt my feelings."

"Well, but—" Andy began helplessly.

"You said we'd be like ships that pass in the night!"

"Oh, my God! Did I say that?"

"You did. I remember every word you said..."

"I didn't think I'd been such an ass. I knew I was giving you up."

"Then why did you do it?"

All at once they were quarreling and still holding tight to each other as if nothing could ever part them now.

"I had to. You don't understand. Meade, I had no money. Not a dime."

"You could have asked me to wait."

"Asked you to wait how long? Tell me, how long *did* you wait? A few weeks. And then you married Sam Havlock."

"Three months. Almost. Never a word from you!"

"I was trying to find a job."

"How could I know that?"

"You ought to have known."

"But you were...so final, Andy! You took my hand and kissed it and then—we were out on the porch at my father's house and I was hurt and mad and—you just left me and almost ran away."

"I did run. I was out of breath by the time I got around the corner. And the reason I ran— No, hold still! I'm not going to let you go again. The reason I ran was that I so wanted to go back to you and ask you to wait until I got a job that would support you."

"Oh, Andy." She put her head on his shoulder.

He held her gently, then less gently, his face against her black hair. "You ought to have known that I couldn't really get along without you. But the next thing I knew, you'd married Sam. So I did wait until I had a decent salary and a little capital, and now you're mine again and you can't do anything about it except tell Sam. Or I'll tell him." He lifted her face, kissed her for a long time and then said, "That's my job. I'll talk to Sam. Tonight. At once."

There was a sharp tug at her elbow; she turned and there was Hoddy, dressed fit to kill; black trousers, pleated white shirt, white dinner jacket.

"Better knock it off," he said agreeably. "There's somebody on the little terrace watching you."

All three of them looked up. There was only the stone railing, a few deck chairs folded back against the mellowed brick wall of the house, no one moving anywhere. Hoddy said, "Oh, I just caught a glimpse of somebody—quick as a crab out of sight, I suppose, when he saw me." He thought and added, "Or she. I really couldn't tell. Anyway, it doesn't much matter, does it? Everyone will soon know—"

"Know what?" Andy snapped.

"Why, that you're home! The whole village knows you and Meade were about to marry when

16

you...that is...you didn't. Your guests are arriving, Meade. Florrie's giving them drinks on the terrace. Aunt Chrissy said you were upstairs. John is doing his butling act in the hall. Sam was just wandering out on the terrace when I came down here. Thought I'd better warn you. Andy, you must come to dinner."

Andy gave an honestly amused laugh. "Not this time, Hoddy."

The years of Meade's marriage to Sam, of playing lady bountiful all over the town and, indeed, the state, accepting all the flowers at prolonged dinners and speechmakings, making a few little speeches herself to supplement Sam's growing interest in public affairs, riding along countless parades for charities, parades for some political goings-on—the whole thing had momentarily faded away as if all the time she had been acting in some facile kind of play. The fact, however, remained: she was Mrs. Sam Havlock.

"No," Meade said, "he can't come, Hoddy. Ever again."

"Meade—" Andy began.

"*Meade!*" Hoddy all but shouted. "What's the idea? Didn't I see you both with my own eyes, acting as if nothing in the world could ever separate you. Good heavens," he blurted out in disgust, "if you didn't look like two lovers everlasting!"

"Shut up," said Meade.

"I won't shut up. I'll...I'll...I don't know what I'll do, but you've got to leave Sam. Only, don't do anything about that right away! I do need some money, just to borrow..." he trailed off with the barest flicker of embarrassment.

Meade wanted to slap him; she also wanted to cry. She said bitterly to Andy, "I *could* have dropped him in the Sound when he was four or so."

Andy grinned slightly. "Pity you didn't."

"Oh, I don't think so," Hoddy said airily. "I

17

could swim like a fish. Besides, she's always loved me. Can't see why, but she does. From my cradle. Now surely you're not going to bring up any nonsense about being Sam's wife. Why, when Andy and I talked in Paris I told him—" He checked himself.

"You didn't tell me you had seen Andy! Just what did you tell him?" Meade asked menacingly.

"Nothing! It's almost time for dinner."

"Hoddy! What did you tell Andy?"

"Well, all right—now don't get mad. I only said something or other, nothing much."

"He said you were a bird in a gilded cage," Andy said flatly.

"You *couldn't* have said such a stupid, silly thing! Not even you, Hoddy!" Meade cried. "Besides, I'm not—" The look in Andy's eyes, too perceptive, too clear, stopped her.

"But the cage *is* gilded," he said softly. "The point is, are you happy in it? That's what I asked Hoddy and after I heard what he said I decided to come here for myself and see you. Now I know—"

"Andy, no, I mustn't let you talk like this. I'm Sam's wife." Her voice shook but she meant it. "I've got to go back to the house. Andy, we'll see each other this summer of course, but no . . . no . . ." She couldn't find the words.

Andy found them. "But no talk of divorce? Don't be silly. Good night, Meade."

He turned around and walked toward the back of the court; there was a door in the fence, near the shed where rackets, nets, all sorts of gear managed to collect; he went on past the kennels, without hearing so much as a peep out of the dogs, which meant that they must be having their evening meal, and vanished into the thicket of pines and hemlocks. Hoddy said casually, "I don't see why you're so determined not to get a divorce. You're not in love with Sam. And he's not in love with you."

18

She stared at Hoddy. "But you...but Sam ...how can you say that—"

"It's true. What's more, you know it and have always known it, I imagine. You married him, sure. All of us were in a bit of a state after father died. No money, no future. Then Sam came along, and obviously you were just the wife he felt his position demanded."

"Hoddy..." It was a choking gulp.

"Sure. He knew all about you. He'd met too many women who were after his money, and though he's not too bright actually, he's bright enough to know that. And there you were. Well-bred, good background, intelligent—sometimes," he added, as if reserving some doubt. "At least you were smart enough to take Sam and his money. You make a pretty showpiece, a happily married couple. Of course, you're not a scrap in love with one another."

"Will you stop that!"

"So get him to let you have a divorce. My guess is he'll not object—not very much, anyway," Hoddy said airily. "If it can be done quietly, no blame in his direction. Sam can easily find somebody else, just as pretty, or almost as pretty, anyway, who would wear his jewels and clothes and be seen with him in public, a conventionally happy married couple."

Once in a while, in an almost childlike way, Hoddy did seem to come up with a profound observation. But he must be wrong. She said soberly, "I'm his wife."

"Better think it over. Andy's not the type to hang around forever. Not the type to be content with a bone now and then, like a stray dog. Incidentally, good thing nobody has let the dogs out. Why you keep those beasts I can't imagine... *Come on!* Glad you've already put on a decent dress. You really do look quite nice, you know. Better than Agnes Garnet; I bet she has a glass of water for lunch and another for dinner. She seems strong enough, but her bones stick out."

Meade wasn't listening. She was moving clumsily, each step was like a mountain to be climbed. It was lucky Hoddy had his arm around her. Darkness was settling down; the waters of the Sound showed only a pinkish glow now, out in the middle of blue-black shadows, a reflection of the rosy tints of the evening sky.

"What did you say about the dogs, Hoddy?" she asked suddenly, coming back to awareness.

"What? Oh, I only said it was a good thing nobody had let out the dogs, at least none of them howled at Andy."

At that moment, however, Marcelline let out a sharp and admonishing yelp which was followed by a shriek of pain from George, her younger offspring. In the silence of the evening both sounds were loud. "But surely the kennel gate is closed," Meade said. "It always is until I let them out myself at night, after the driveway gate is closed."

"Well," Hoddy said, rubbing his chin reluctantly, "I'll go and make sure. I can't say without a certain trepidation."

"They won't hurt you. Look out for Marcelline, though. The vet took a cyst out of her shoulder yesterday and she's still a little snappish."

"A lethal menagerie! *Kerry blues!* As soon kill anybody as look at them."

"You don't have to worry unless they stand very still and their eyes turn sort of purple," she said absently. "Anyway, they won't hurt you. Just be sure the kennel gate is locked."

"So they won't chew my leg off. Famous last words," Hoddy said gloomily and slouched down the steps again.

Twilight was lowering quickly over the Sound; the tide kept coming in, slowly, as it always did, and inexorably.

Blue Water Cove was in its way typical of old

and dignified Long Island towns; it even strove to keep up the village atmosphere in spite of the enormous new houses which gradually managed to inject themselves into what, not too long ago, had been pasture land, or merely land and trees. These houses luckily were always set well away from the little village, for all of the owners seemed enthusiastic in their efforts to conform to what they felt Blue Water Cove had always been. Therefore perhaps the unpretentious little town had gained, to outsiders, an aura, a reputation of exclusiveness. Blue Water Cove in one's address meant something, especially to these rich and indeed very helpful newcomers. It was they who had built the golf course and clubhouse, politely remote from the center of the village. Sam alone had paid for the village swimming pool because the water in the Sound was not always conducive to swimming, but that, too, had been built far enough away so it wouldn't infringe on the little village, and yet the young people could bicycle to it easily. Or drive. Suddenly one effect of the village's growing, if unobtrusive, population was the increasing number of ancient and clattering automobiles. Hoddy's was one of them.

But many names besides Sam's, which was included in the village tax rolls, were prominent names. Sam Havlock, of course, was known all over the state, not only in the Cove.

Meade felt as if she hadn't the strength to crawl up the long flight of steps; she needed a little time to sit on the bench and look at the quiet water, quiet yet moving stealthily inward. However, she pulled herself together; she was the hostess. She clung to the railing, which felt cold to her hand.

Above there was the glimmer of the hurricane candles, already alight, placed on the table in the wide curve of the upper terrace.

The scene as she reached the top of the steps was almost exactly as she had known it would be.

21

Florrie was flirting around in her most successful role as French maid, and Meade had a sudden impulse to tell her to go and do something about her black-rimmed eyes. John was visible in the hall, where Sam had yielded to present-day demands and had had a lavish bar installed. On the terrace stood a long glass-topped table; around the candles, which gave forth a mellow glow, there were silver and glass, olives and cheese—this time also caviar and smoked salmon, Sam's favorites. He had evidently taken his drink from where she had left it on the table because it was gone, but Sam was not on the terrace. Agnes came to meet her, looking almost thin enough to justify Hoddy's speculation about her diet. But undeniably chic, even on the tennis court, where she was an untiring and skillful player. Always chic, with her shining cap of light hair, not a strand out of place, her full mouth, her serene eyes. She greeted Meade with her usual quiet charm and Meade was momentarily thankful that Agnes never expected much in the way of talk, to say nothing of polite gush from anybody.

Brice came to Meade and gave her a peck on the cheek. Brice was Sam's closest friend; he was older than Sam but they had been friends since Sam's school days. Brice had had a little money to start with but had built himself up so quickly and successfully in his law practice that he had in the past few years turned his attention to politics—and that again so quickly and successfully that he was running for governor. He always kept himself in good trim; he was dark and good-looking, but, Meade had often thought, amused, if any woman sought to lure him away from his wife, she would be soundly defeated. His devotion to Agnes and their two children, and Agnes' obvious devotion to him, sometimes touched Meade with envy.

Agnes said, "How wonderfully well you are looking, Meade. This place agrees with you."

"Agrees with all of us," said Brice.

Both Brice and Agnes had tall, ice-dappled drinks in their hands. Brice turned to Aunt Chrissy. "Can I get you something, Miss Chrissy?"

Aunt Chrissy was seated in a woven rattan chair with a high spreading back which gave a queenly endorsement of her always queenly presence. However, at the moment she was in a matriarchal mood, for she had pulled out a nondescript mass of blue yarn that may have been begun sometime in the past but certainly had never ended. It was a favorite maneuver of hers when she wished to impress Meade or Hoddy with her position as their aunt and authority. True, she had lived with Meade's and Hoddy's father ever since the death of her husband some ten or twelve years before, but neither of them now paid much more than polite attention to her commands.

She looked up from the mass of knitting and said, "Yes, Brice, I'll take a little drink, thanks. So mild, so sweet. Such a dear name—Southern Comfort." Aunt Chrissy knew perfectly well that her favorite drink was not exactly like iced tea or a cola, but she stubbornly pretended it had no alcoholic content whatever. Agnes smiled. Brice muttered "Southern dynamite" under his breath, and Aunt Chrissy added rather sharply, "Where is Sam?"

Where was Sam?

He wasn't on the terrace. "But he *was* here," Agnes said. "Just a moment ago."

Aunt Chrissy's perfectly coiffed white head nodded. "Oh, he was here, sitting on the balustrade. I dropped a stitch and looked down at my knitting, and then when I looked up he was gone."

"Went into the house," Brice said. "He'll be back. Now then." He gave Aunt Chrissy her drink and settled himself in a long wicker chair.

Florrie gave a whisk of her short black skirt. She

23

did not intend to be overlooked if she could help it. "Mr. Garnet, Mr. Havlock did not go into the house. He took his drink, just as he always does. Then he said the sun was over the yardarm, always says that too. He was sitting on the balustrade when I turned to pass sandwiches—"

"He's in the house," Meade said. "He'll be back out in a moment. Hoddy will be here, too. He went to make sure the dogs were locked up."

Unexpectedly Aunt Chrissy said, "But I tell you, he *was* sitting right there." She pointed with a knitting needle to a spot near her on the wide balustrade. "But then he was gone. Just gone."

Brice said, "He'll turn up. John!" he called toward the open door.

John appeared at once. Like Florrie, and for the same reason, he really overdid his domestic role. "You called, sir?" the black coat, the striped trousers, the winged collar, Meade thought idly, the very trappings, maybe even taken from the theater wardrobe, of the role in which Sam had seen him act and had hired him and Florrie to pursue their careers in his own house. To do them justice, they had played excellent roles as servants. Unconventional, indeed unusual, but in Sam's way he had got what he wanted; he had a butler and housemaid.

Now John's "Sir" was the very acme of the trained, polite butler.

But he had not seen Mr. Havlock since he went through the hall and out onto the terrace. Yes, John had been at the bar the whole time. He had an impression that Mr. Havlock had taken his drink, gone to sit on the balustrade and as usual said something about the sun being over the yardarm. Then, John went on conscientiously, Mr. and Mrs. Garnet had arrived and Miss Chrissy had asked him to get out the special bottle of Southern Comfort he kept for her and—well, that was all.

24

No, he had no idea where Mr. Havlock had gone but certainly not back into the house because he had been at the bar and would have seen him.

So where was Sam? He hadn't gone down the steps toward the tennis court. Meade herself would have met him. Florrie contributed to that fact fully, taking all the spotlight she could get. He would have had to pass her and he hadn't.

"He had his drink in his hand. He sat right there." Again Aunt Chrissy stabbed at the spot with her knitting needles. Suddenly her fine features turned chalk-white. She dropped the mass of knitting; she clutched the arm of her chair for an instant and then rose and walked steadily to the balustrade. She look down. "I always said sometime somebody would fall..." She stopped.

There was a kind of swish and tap of heels. Agnes' perfume was like a cloud around Meade. All of them leaned over and looked down and down, through gathering gloom, past a helter-skelter of boulders and scraggly pines and tangled shrubbery, way down to the reeds along the Sound which the incoming tide was moving sluggishly, looked down to where a white flaccid hand moved idly, stirring a little with the tide.

Hoddy had come from somewhere. He shouted "It's Sam!" and dashed down the steps. Meade, following him, stumbled in her haste and was caught by Brice, who was behind her. Somehow all at once they were all down there by the water.

Meade was barely conscious of the wetness around her ankles as she edged into the reeds. Hoddy and Brice and John pulled her husband out of the water.

"My God, he's gone!" Brice said.

"Let me try." Hoddy was astride Sam's body, pushing and letting up, pushing and letting up. Aunt Chrissy was only halfway down the steps. She screamed, "I'll call the doctor!"

25

It was the most sensible thing anybody could have done, but it was too late because Sam Havlock was dead.

"Why," Aunt Chrissy said later, "it's as if somebody pulled him over backward, just pulled him like a doll and dropped him there and he didn't fight, he didn't yell. I didn't even notice his feet go over."

Two

That was after the Coast Guard boats, the police launches and the Blue Cove water ambulance had come; that was after the dashing lights of the boats had gone and only a circle of light outlined the place where Sam had been found. That was at last extinguished and the police came to the house. Hoddy, Meade thought but wasn't sure, had contrived to get Agnes, Aunt Chrissy and her up to the terrace again. But from there they had watched the whole dashing cluster of lights, the dark hurriedly moving figures of men. Away back at the side of the house, between the front entrance and the tennis court, there was a constant background of yelping and snarling from the dogs; all these strange cars invading their territory and they didn't like it.

When the lights of the boats had gone, someone,

Agnes probably, led the way into the house and turned on lights in the long living room with its sparkling chandeliers and the great mirror above the fireplace. Here the medical examiner came over briefly to introduce himself. Dr. Abernathy wore horn-rimmed glasses and was busy taking notes in a thick black-covered notebook. He nodded absently as they gave their names, and addressed himself to Meade sympathetically and kindly, asking for her permission to do a post-mortem on Sam's body. "You see, he was not a patient of mine. I can't give a death certificate. It's the law."

After a moment Meade took in the sense of his words. She nodded. "Yes, yes, of course I see that."

"Especially when it's an accident," Agnes said. "Now doctor, I doubt if Mrs Havlock has anything like a sleeping pill. Do you think you could give her something? She's had a frightful shock."

The doctor nodded. "Certainly." He carried his little black bag with him, too; he opened it, selected a bottle, shook out three or four capsules into a small envelope and gave them to Agnes. "Don't let her take them all at once. I gather you are a close friend. If I might suggest..."

Agnes was always quick on the uptake. "Oh yes, I'll stay with her tonight. Her aunt—"

At the word "aunt," Chrissy bridled; she sat up very straight, a completely empty glass of Southern Comfort upside down in her hand. "I am perfectly capable of sheeing to my family, unnerstan?"

This ought to have shocked Meade; any other time it would have been a hilarious kind of joke between her and Hoddy. Now Aunt Chrissy could take the whole bottle of Southern Comfort to bed with her if she liked and nobody would care.

"Agnes, I'm here too," Hoddy said with unusual firmness.

Agnes looked at him seriously and after a
28

moment said, "Of course you are, Hoddy. I'll go along home, then. But if you should want me, just phone."

Dr. Abernathy nodded briskly. Agnes and the doctor were escorted to the door by Hoddy; sometimes he used very good sense—when he put his mind to it.

He didn't use any a moment later, for suddenly he came bursting back into the room, pulling Andrew Brooke with him. Behind them came a fat man in a dark suit and neat white shirt, bald-headed and saggy-chinned, with very bright eyes. Meade knew him well; Chief Haggerty of the Blue Water Cove police. Following him was a younger man in the blue uniform of the Cove police.

Meade's heart thudded. Andy ought not to be anywhere here. An atavistic instinct told her that, as it might have warned her of danger, not from Andy but from the police.

And indeed her instinct was right. Andy said, "I'm sorry, Meade. I've just heard the news. Fact is, I saw the water ambulance leaving..."

Chief Haggerty gave Andy half a grin and half a frown. "Remember me, Andy?"

Andy's eyes gleamed momentarily. "Question is, do you remember chasing me off the sidewalk on my roller skates?"

Chief Haggerty nodded. "I also remember having to send the Coast Guard to pick you up out of the Sound."

"I'm afraid I remember only too well the fine you gave me. At least you called it a fine."

This time the chief really grinned. "You needed every lick of it. Took two officers to get you out of the water. You were nearly winded."

"Well, thanks anyway for saving my life."

The chief sobered. "How did you happen to come here tonight?"

"Saw the commotion and came to see what had happened," Andy replied promptly. "All those cars

29

and everything. I'm staying at Cousin Isabel's down the street." Cousin Isabel was, in fact, some remote relative of his mother's.

The chief's eyes twinkled just slightly. "Miss Isabel didn't send you, then?"

Andy permitted himself a very slight twinkle, too. "Not exactly. Of course, she is naturally interested in knowing what goes on." He became very grave. "What did happen?"

"Didn't Hoddy tell you?"

"He said Sam Havlock had fallen from the terrace and drowned. I came in to hear how it happened."

Again Meade felt an uneasy quiver of something like danger. Sam's death was an accident; it couldn't be anything else. But suppose—just suppose someone knew that she and Andy had met and Andy wanted her to ask Sam for a divorce. Just suppose—she pushed the ugly little fear back. Brice Garnet came swiftly through the group of men. "Meade, Agnes is in the car. Now, if you want me to stay—"

"*I'll* be here," Hoddy said, bristling again at the implicit insult to his masculine strength and good sense.

"Yes." Brice's tanned face had taken on a grayish tinge. "Yes, certainly, Hoddy." His eyes narrowed as he spotted Andy. "Why, it's—it must be Andrew Brooke! I didn't know you were home!"

"I haven't been here long." Andy shook hands with Brice. "I still don't know what happened. They just said that Sam Havlock fell from the terrace and drowned."

"Seems like it," said Chief Haggerty. "Medical examiner will say just what happened."

"You mean"—Andy looked puzzled—"a heart attack or . . . or something?"

"Or something," said the chief.

Brice frowned. "Now, look here, Chief, Sam was in perfect health. It had to be an accident."

"We don't know anything yet," Haggerty said, whirled smartly, and followed by his subordinate, marched out of the room. Their footsteps resounded on the parquet floor of the hall.

Hoddy scowled. "Now what did he mean by that? Good God, there wasn't any other way for Sam to fall. Nobody pushed him. He wouldn't let himself be pushed. He didn't knock himself over intentionally."

There was a heavy but thoughtful silence. Meade thought that for an instant Andy moved toward her but then stopped himself.

Somebody had to do or say something; the heavy silence was unbearable. Meade rose and half stumbled toward the stairs. "I'll go...I'm tired...I'm..." She knew she was making no sense. She found the steps by instinct and was suddenly, thankfully, in her own room, the door closed as if against an enemy. And there was a possible enemy. Suppose the police said Sam was murdered and Andy had killed him?

Of course that was nonsense.

It was not entirely nonsense the next morning when John brought her coffee. He had dropped his butlerish airs; he was simply a miserably unhappy out-of-work actor. He put down the tray with silver coffeepot and delicate china cup and then without a word of apology subsided into a small chair, so small that his knees stuck up, an awkward pose no professional actor would have adopted intentionally for an instant. "Mrs. Havlock, I mean Madam, the police are here and they keep asking me and asking me who pushed Mr. Havlock over the balustrade. Madam,"—he wrung his hands with an actor's gesture of anguish—"I keep telling them nobody pushed him. He must have fallen. But he didn't yell; he didn't scream or call for help or anything..."

Meade tried to speak calmly. "It was an

31

accident, John. He simply fell backwards."

"But that policeman says he would have struggled or called for help. He says"—his whole face became even more miserable—"somebody on the terrace could have pushed him so hard and fast that he didn't have time to yell or— But that doesn't make sense, Madam, not to me. Nobody could have pushed Mr. Havlock off the balustrade; he wouldn't have let anybody do that. Of course"—a hopeful gleam came into his mobile face—"he may have thought he could catch hold of some of the shrubbery or something, but that doesn't seem reasonable. You see, what makes it so terrible—there were only me and Florrie, your Aunt Chrissy and Mr. and Mrs. Garnet anywhere near the terrace at the time he fell." He thought for a moment, pale eyes vacant, and added, "That's a very strange thing, you know, Madam. Like spirits, if you understand me."

She pushed back her hair. "You mean his drink?"

"No, no. I mean...spirits"—he waved one hand—"from the outer world."

Meade lifted her cup of coffee which he had poured and thought for a while. "John," she said at last, "I honestly don't think some strange outer force came swooping down on our terrace and pushed him over to drown."

He was doubtful. "You can't deny the fact that he just disappeared into thin air with five people right around him, and your aunt says she didn't even see his feet go over."

Hoddy knocked and came in. "My God, Meade," he said with brotherly candor, "you look like death warmed over. Oh, sorry, I've said the wrong thing. Anyway, I brought you some breakfast. You need more than coffee. Thank you just the same, John. Now Meade, here's scrambled eggs, bacon and toast. Get some inside you. We've got a bad day ahead of us."

John uncrumpled himself from the chair but couldn't quite assume his butler role. "I've been telling her."

"Thank you, Hoddy. I can't eat—"

"What's the matter with him?" Hoddy asked briskly when John shambled out the door.

"He thinks...he suggested the spirits pulled Sam down. Spirits from the outer world, he said."

Hoddy looked horrified. "You mean—that is, he means that something unseen by the rest of the people on the terrace simply whirled down and whisked Sam over the balustrade and wouldn't let him yell or try to help himself? Is the fellow in his right mind? I told Sam he shouldn't employ out-of-work actors."

"Take that tray away."

"Eat," Hoddy said, sat down on the bed and scooped up a forkful of eggs which he thrust in her mouth.

So she ate, swallowing hard, until she firmly closed her mouth and refused more. Nevertheless, the food and the coffee were beginning to put some strength into her. She hadn't eaten since—oh, since when? Luncheon the day before, which had consisted of a sandwich at the village drugstore while she waited for the vet to remove the cyst from Marcelline's shoulder.

"Now," Hoddy said, "you're a new woman. Let's face the following facts. One outstanding fact is this." His face grew very young and solemn. "They've done an autopsy, not complete yet. They have to send some of the—some of the things to a laboratory somewhere. They think it very unlikely that Sam could have had a sudden heart attack or a stroke. They are very definite about that. They can't figure, though, how he just went over the balustrade, people all around him, yet nobody saw it happen, he didn't yell or make any sound, he just vanished. I'll tell you what I think." He cast an eye at the door, went to make sure it was closed, came back and said, "What I think is that some guy dropped a noose, a lariat, around his neck, choked him at once so he couldn't cry out and just pulled him softly over. Maybe it knocked him out—they didn't say anything about any special bruise on his head but that could have happened—and then the guy got away through the woods. Maybe even had a boat somewhere near. How does that sound to you?"

She was feeling more like herself. "It sounds like something you made up. It's even more fanciful than a murderous spirit from outer space. Really, Hoddy!"

"Makes perfect sense to me. Actually, when you come to think of it, it's the only way he could have vanished just like that. Florrie and John and the Garnets all standing around the table with drinks and appetizers. Aunt Chrissy snarled up with her knitting. And without a sound Sam is just—just gone. To his death!" he added dramatically.

He did have the grace to look rather stricken after that. "Sorry, Meade. But you must admit it's a strange kind of thing to happen. The police want to talk to you. So get yourself together. Or if you want me to, I'll tell them you're in no condition to talk to them."

She took a long breath. "I'll have to sometime, Hoddy. Better get it over with."

A slight air of evasion came upon him. "Maybe I ought to phone Brice."

"Brice? Why?"

"Your rights. Have a lawyer with you at all times. Meade, really, you are such a baby about some things. Don't you know that when a man is murdered—"

"He wasn't murdered!"

"Well, then, a sudden death which nobody can explain. The first suspects are his wife and anybody else who would profit by his death. I should say that you will profit by enough money to
34

make the whole police force point its collective finger at you. Especially," he added, "if anybody tells them about the little scene between you and Andy Brooke down at the tennis court."

Instantly, as if a curtain had risen displaying an incredibly frightening scene, all the implications of Hoddy's words overwhelmed her. She shoved back the tray. "I'll get ready."

"Better pick out a very simple dress and no make-up. Remember, you are the bereaved widow."

"Oh, get out!" Meade erupted.

The sting of the shower, alternately hot and cold, revived her a little. Without thinking, she followed Hoddy's advice: a plain cotton dress, hair brushed neatly back. Surely they wouldn't, they couldn't, nobody could suspect Andy of—well, doing what? Getting Sam somehow, who could guess how, off the balustrade without being seen, then lower him into the rising tide of the Sound and leave him to drown.

It was impossible.

Oddly, for just an instant, she remembered that Hoddy had said he thought someone was watching her and Andy from the little terrace, just above the tennis court. Suppose it was true.

The chief of police, together with an officer in blue uniform and a stiff-looking bony little man with sharp gray eyes, were waiting in the spacious library, which Sam used to call his study. Chief Haggerty said "Good morning," the young man in uniform seemed to bow rather awkwardly, and the little man with gray eyes came to meet her. "I expect you remember me, Mrs. Havlock."

She did, of course; he was a member of the vast law firm that dealt with Sam's affairs. She fumbled for his name and finally remembered it. "Yes, Mr. Bacon."

He had taken her hand in a dry clasp. "I do indeed regret the tragic necessity of my visit. I

35

thought—that is, it was thought by my firm—that one of us should see you as soon as possible. It was kind of your brother to inform our office of your husband's death so soon."

"Hoddy did that? I never thought of it."

"Naturally not. In any event, we'd have seen the newspapers."

Chief Haggerty said quietly that he couldn't do anything about the reporters. "It's their job. There was one at the hospital last night, so—"

Mr. Bacon interrupted smoothly. "Of course, of course. Now then, you must be informed about something of your husband's affairs, Mrs. Havlock. It was determined that I should come to Blue Water Cove for this reason."

Meade was still astonished that Hoddy had made such a quick and expedient gesture. She sat down and motioned for Mr. Bacon and the other two to take chairs. They did so, Mr. Bacon adjusting the knifelike creases over his bony knees and glancing at Chief Haggerty. "Do you wish what I have to say—very little actually, but still..."

Chief Haggerty interpreted this and said firmly, "Anything about Mr. Havlock's affairs is of interest to the police, Mr. Bacon."

Mr. Bacon's bright gray eyes shot the chief a piercing glance. "Are you thinking of suicide?"

The chief heaved a troubled sigh. "To tell you the truth, we don't know what to think. Suicide? It's an alternative, certainly."

There was a short silence. "And you, Mrs. Havlock?" the lawyer said.

Meade nodded. "It's all right, Mr. Bacon. Anything..."

"I see. H'mm—well, I think I can condense this. In short, we drew Mr. Havlock's will shortly after his marriage to you. He listed his property—unusual, really, but very thoughtful of him; his shares in the Emmeline Holding Company, his entire estate, including this house, his apartment in New York, his yacht. It was extremely wise of Mr. Havlock to go into such detail. A great help to us in implementing his will."

She had not thought of a will. There had been too many more important things to think of. This, of course, was why Hoddy had taken it upon himself to inform the lawyers' office of Sam's death. Hoddy, at least, had shown himself practical and prompt.

She nodded again.

Mr. Bacon made a tent of his small bony hands and eyed it. "He left his entire estate to his wife," he said flatly.

"Oh," said Meade.

He gave her a reproving glance. "It is a very large estate, as I understand it. Values do fluctuate, times change, income varies. But we believe that when all the reports from the diverse companies forming the Emmeline Holding Company are in, you will be a very rich young woman. Allowing even for inheritance taxes."

"Oh," she said again. But of course, Sam had been rich.

"Yes." Mr. Bacon's thin lips almost smiled. "We must have all Mr. Havlock's interests thoroughly audited. That may take time. Yes. Considerable time perhaps, although we—I mean, my firm will make every effort to expedite these reports. Yes. In the meantime you must draw on us for anything in the way of cash you might require. Better send the account of all your expenses to our office. Naturally, we are to act as executors. I am personally delegated as one of them. The other two are representatives of the Emmeline Holding Company."

"I see," Meade said in a small voice. "Yes. Yes, certainly."

"We have information as to the banks which he used and, I believe, his safe-deposit boxes. His personal secretary, Miss Bellamy, is informed as to many of these things. I telephoned your husband's New York office as soon as I could this morning. As I expect you know, he kept a very small staff there. Miss Bellamy, I understand, is on vacation. In fact"—his dry tone seemed to disapprove of Miss Bellamy's lack of foresight in view of her employer's unexpected death—"she has started on a safari. I am told that she was in Nairobi last night and is now on her way to a place called Treetops. All this in order to watch African animals in luxurious surroundings. When we can get in touch with her, we shall be able to find information as to every item of your husband's estate and then eventually be able to send his will to probate."

"Oh," Meade said again.

"Various formalities, yes. These need not concern you. Now, as I say, values do fluctuate. But in my opinion, judging from your husband's will, there should be about three"—his eyes narrowed speculatively—"yes, there should be about three for you."

Three what? she thought vaguely. It appeared all of them expected her to say something, so she said falteringly, "I know nothing of Sam's business."

"You know he was a very rich man," said Mr. Bacon.

"Why, I—why, yes of course!" His charities given with so lavish a hand! Her mind flashed on to the big duplex apartment on Fifth Avenue in New York; there were paintings worth a fortune in themselves; there was a yacht which they had rarely used. There were employees who must be paid. "We never talked of money," she said flatly. "Except sometimes when he was debating some bequest like—oh, a new wing for a hospital, or some additions to an art museum. But of course I knew Sam is—was very rich. He gave so much to charities and...he was very generous with me."

There was another silence in the room. Haggerty's eyes were almost closed on whatever thought he had. His young subordinate was less experienced at concealing his interest.

Mr. Bacon made a careful tent again with his fingers, and contemplating it, said, "Yes, I should say at least three."

Three? Meade thought again, puzzled.

The chief of police couldn't stand it. "Three hundred thousand?"

Mr. Bacon turned on him with blank astonishment. "My dear sir!"

The young policeman was red in the face but said daringly, "Three million!"

Mr. Bacon said gently, "Three hundred million."

Meade cried, "I can't—you must be mistaken—there isn't that much!"

"I think when things are settled you'll find I'm not far off," said Mr. Bacon.

But there isn't that much money in the world, Meade thought, in a wave of something like hysteria, clutching at the arm of her chair. Certainly not for me!

Mr. Bacon added, "Of course that would be subject to very heavy taxes, I'm afraid. Also the present assets of the Emmeline Holding Company and of Mr. Havlock must be audited and suitably appraised. This is only my quick and conservative opinion."

Three

Hoddy came in and put his hand down hard on her shoulder. "My sister is still in a state of shock," he said. "May we leave business matters till later? There are some arrangements to be made and—I'm sure you'll understand. But it was very kind, very thoughtful of you to come out here at once to advise my sister. I'm sure she is most grateful for it."

His hand pressed down on Meade's shoulder. She said yes, yes, it was very kind, and thanked Mr. Bacon, who shook her unsteady hand and told her that he would be seeing her again, that he would see that records of Mr. Havlock's entire estate would be assembled for her inspection.

At the door, however, he turned and fastened a needle-sharp gaze upon Chief Haggerty. "You said something about an 'alternative,' speaking of suicide as a reason for Mr. Havlock's death. Are there—I should say, is there another alternative?"

"There may be," the chief said curtly. "I'll come to the door with you."

To explain the circumstances of Sam's death, Meade thought, but those circumstances could not so far be explained.

Mr. Bacon gave a reserved kind of bow in Meade's direction. The chief and his cohort went out with him, and someone closed the door.

Hoddy sighed. "Now the chief is telling him the whole story as he knows it. I hope this doesn't foul up your inheritance. But then"—his face brightened—"of course it couldn't; the law says only a murderer cannot profit by the murder."

"Hoddy!" Another thought occurred to her. "You phoned Mr. Bacon."

"Certainly I did."

"So you knew the name of the lawyers—the firm."

Hoddy nodded. "I suppose anyone could know that. Anyway, I did, and I phoned because I thought you ought to know right away where you stand about money. Anything wrong with that?"

"I guess not."

Hoddy said thoughtfully, "Three hundred million dollars!"

"You were listening at the door."

He didn't bother to deny it. "Three hundred *million!*"

"It's too much. I don't need—"

"Oh, you'll find it very useful," Hoddy said cynically. "But there's one thing you've got to be careful about: don't look too cheerful."

"Cheerful? I don't feel cheerful."

"Three hundred million for certain!" Hoddy almost rolled the words on his tongue as if tasting them. "Never mind the taxes. How could anybody not feel cheerful about that! And all because of an accident. Just don't look too cheerful, I told you.

42

People will say you had a motive for pushing Sam over the balustrade. Not," he added, "that they're not thinking it already."

"Hoddy, it *was* an accident. There he was, with people around him—"

"And he vanishes. Falls down that rocky slope, if you can call it a slope, straight into the Sound and drowns. He wasn't drunk. He'd had only that one hideous drink you mixed for him. There's no sense to it. But with that much money involved, do you think for one minute that the police aren't going to say you had a motive for getting rid of him?"

"*Hoddy!*"

"All right. Now, pull yourself together and listen to me. The police are going to question you, ask you everything they can think of. Nobody can say what happened to Sam, but all the same, just in case, the police are going to treat it very seriously—"

"In case—"

"—In case it should turn out to be murder. That's what old Bacon was thinking."

"It can't be murder!"

"I don't see how. But all the same..." He sat down on the arm of her chair. "That money is big enough motive for anybody. And if anybody at all knows that you saw Andy just before Sam went down in the Sound, there you have another motive and a big one. Emotional reaction on your part or on Andy's..."

"I wasn't on the terrace when Sam fell! Neither was Andy!"

"Don't argue. There's no time. Just listen. You are not to admit having seen Andy before dinner at all. You are not to admit that he so much as mentioned divorce. Sam's money, his name, everything, could turn this into a big case—you know the newspapers. Good God, I don't want them to arrest you for murder."

"It wasn't murder," Meade said again, but weakly. Could Hoddy possibly be right?

Someone knocked politely. It was again the chief of police and his attendant policeman. "May we talk to you now, Mrs. Havlock?"

"Certainly, Chief," Meade replied.

She had known Chief Haggerty for most of her life; he had changed slowly over the years from a spry young traffic cop, guaranteed to catch the most daring speeder, to a bulky, authoritative, gray-haired figure with deep-set eyes, which saw a great deal, and a patient but tenacious manner. He showed a definite lack of cringing respect for anybody who might become the possessor of so shocking a sum as three hundred million dollars. For this Spartan disregard of riches, as well as for his known character, Meade respected him. She also felt again just a twinge of something like fear. He knew that Andy had returned. He had seen and talked to him. Andy and money; oh yes, it could be said that there were motives for Sam's murder. But he hadn't been murdered.

"I'm sorry to trouble you this morning," Chief Haggerty said, "really sorry. But there are some puzzling things about your husband's death. I've been explaining this to your lawyer. As I told him, the first report of the autopsy shows no indication whatever of anything say, like a stroke or a heart attack. Had he ever showed any signs of such a thing? I mean, any illness at all, dizziness?"

"No, nothing."

She thought of Sam, big, blond, with a wide smile showing perfect white teeth. Like the chief, he had gained a little weight over the years and dieted strenuously when he thought of it. He never stinted his energies when it came to any occasion for public welfare. He even delivered his speeches, which she knew that the very intelligent and discreet Miss Bellamy had prepared for him, in such a frank way that he could have been

44

speaking, face to face, with any one person in the audience. The whole state had reason to mourn so generous a man.

The chief said slowly, "There are several things I can't seem to get clear in my mind. Now tell me again just where you were when your husband fell."

"I don't know. I had been down at the tennis court. I was coming up the steps. There's a bench at the landing and I stopped there for a while and just looked out over the Sound. It was getting dark. The tide was coming in. Then I came on up the steps and someone asked where Sam—"

"Who asked that?"

"Why, I don't remember. Yes, I do. It was my Aunt Chrissy. She said he'd been sitting on the terrace, beside her."

"So she said. She said she didn't see him fall. Didn't even feel him move. Nobody seems to have seen him fall. Yet there were five people on that terrace."

"I didn't see Sam at all then," Meade said. "I suppose the others were—oh, around the table where there were drinks or just looking out over the Sound or talking. That's what they were doing when I came up the steps. And Aunt Chrissy said, 'Where is Sam?' Then we—"

"Yes, then what did you do?"

"It's confusing..."

"I can see that," Haggerty said rather too dryly.

Hoddy said quickly, "I was locking up the dogs. I didn't see Sam. Of course, he must have been on the terrace then."

Meade said, "John said he couldn't have gone back into the house without being seen, I mean by John, and then we looked..." She lowered her head.

Haggerty said with sincere apology in his voice, "I am sorry, Mrs. Havlock. But it'll help things later, if you don't mind."

Hoddy's clasp on her shoulder seemed to stiffen. "What do you mean 'later'?"

Haggerty straightened his shoulders and answered bluntly, man to man, "If we find evidence of murder."

"He couldn't have been murdered!" Meade cried. "Nobody would have murdered him. Nobody had any reason to murder him, or *any way* to murder him."

"There, there, Meade—I mean Mrs. Havlock. I keep forgetting you are grown up and married..."

"My name is still Meade," she said absently.

He gave her an equally absent nod. "It'll be several days before we get the complete findings from the laboratory."

"But," Hoddy said after a pause, "you want to get all the information you can get, just in case."

"You can call it that," Haggerty said. He looked troubled, yet stubborn. "It's so very unusual. Man sitting on his own terrace, just disappears, found moments later—how many moments nobody seems to know—dead. Drowned. Right below his own house. Didn't call for help. He was a fine swimmer; the only explanation for his drowning is that he may have knocked his head on that slope going down from the terrace to the Sound. Rock and shrubbery, a rough descent. But still—no, I can't understand it." He pushed one hand over bushy, graying hair and said abruptly, "And when there's something I don't understand, it bothers me. Man killed, five people around. Mrs. Havlock—that is, Meade—you've known your husband for a long time?"

"Of course, Chief, you know that. Since—well, since he finished school and came back here to live. He didn't stay here for long at a time, but it always seemed his home. Then, as he grew older, and I grew older too, he began to take me out for rides and to the movies, and sometimes to New York for

46

dinner and a show. And then we were married. Three years ago."

"Yes, I remember. Big wedding. Invited me, too. Like Sam Havlock to remember me. That was just about the time Andy Brooke left town, wasn't it?"

Steady, Meade. "Yes. Perhaps a little later."

"Perhaps," the chief said thoughtfully. "Well, well. Nice to know that Andy has come back for a visit. I hear he's getting along well. Always knew there was good stuff in that boy. Now, let me see. Your father died before your marriage, didn't he?"

"Oh yes. You knew my father, Chief! Dr. Forrest."

"Sure. Cottage down there in the Cove. Professor of something or other, nice old party. Everybody was sorry when he died. That was not long before your wedding."

"Six weeks before," Meade said, sad even now. Perhaps if her father had not died just then, she might not have married Sam, at least not so soon.

"M'm, yes. I'd forgotten exactly. Relatives?"

"My brother here, Hoddy. And you know there's my Aunt Chrissy Halsey, a widow, my father's sister. She lived with us." Meade's thoughts flew back to the quiet days in the book-lined cottage where her father had serenely passed the last days of his long and, in a sense, rewarding life. After his teaching career had ended, pupils still came to him from near and far, relating their exploits, asking his advice or simply basking in the wise charm he unconsciously exerted. Hoddy basked in it a little too much; Hoddy simply could not see any reason to do anything he didn't really want to do. So when her father died and his retirement pay died with him, Hoddy was still not interested in preparing himself to earn money in any possible profession. Much as she loved Hoddy, she had realized that he must find his own way.

But then Sam had given him money; when

Hoddy hinted, Sam readily put his hand in his pockets, always generous as if he didn't care, as if money were only paper.

Sam was never a clearly definable personality. Perhaps she hadn't tried hard enough to understand him. That was her own fault, then, because she couldn't stop loving Andy. She had gone through the entire three years of marriage to Sam like a doll, wound up to do the proper and agreeable things, but her real heart and soul, her whole human instinct simply did not mesh with Sam's. Yes, she could blame herself; yet she had tried. She had been Sam's wife and owed him respect.

Chief Haggerty said, "I understand you and Andy Brooke had quite a talk down on the tennis court just before you came up to the terrace. Is that right?"

Hoddy made some move and Meade said quickly, afraid he was going to attempt to lie in her behalf, "Yes, we did. He and Hoddy had been playing tennis. I went down to see him. He's been away a long time."

Hoddy burst out, "Who told you that, Chief?"

The chief eyed him good-naturedly, but searchingly too. "That man who works for you. The actor you call the butler—John Elwell. When I questioned him about the whole affair he volunteered the information. But, Meade, the whole town knows that you and Andy were engaged at one time. Was it a friendly talk with Andy?"

"Yes." Had John seen them embracing, kissing, had he heard what they said? She wasn't to know, for the chief said, "Well, it's nice of you to give me all this time, Meade—I mean Mrs. Havlock."

"I told you, Meade will do," Meade said, wishing for an instant that she were the carefree teenager he had always called Meade and had once given a hearty talking-to about parking her father's ancient car in a no-parking zone.

The chief smiled, touched his forehead as if he

48

wore a hat and went away. The young officer hustled after the chief.

Hoddy groaned and let his lanky body collapse into one of the great leather armchairs. "John saw that! How much did he see? And *hear*?"

"It couldn't have been much," Meade said resolutely. "Really, Hoddy. He had to come into the house and see to drinks and things. But did you see *him* on the tennis-court terrace?"

Hoddy sighed. "I'm not even sure I saw anybody. Just a kind of flicker."

"Andy had gone before I came up to join the others. That is certain. He wasn't near the upper terrace until he arrived after the ambulance boat had gone."

Hoddy leaned forward, bony elbows on bony knees. "The way I see it," he said with an air of great perspicacity, "is this: the police suspect something but don't know what to suspect. Plain as the nose on your face. All those questions ..." He sprang up. "Good God, Meade, did you have any notion that Sam was so rich?"

"Of course I knew he had money, but he never discussed business affairs with me."

"I never dreamed he was *that* rich," Hoddy said ruefully. "Why, I could have had—" He stopped. "Sorry, Meade. It's just a kind of—well, you can't say blow exactly, but it *is* a surprise. You'll be a rich woman, no matter what."

"Oh, Hoddy, don't talk about it!"

Hoddy thought for a moment, a puzzled look on his face. "You know, Meade, sometimes I had the feeling that though Sam gave to charity all the time, it was as if his heart wasn't in it. I don't know how to say it, but it was as if he had no real interest in the cause itself. I can't say what, but as if something else was on his mind. Funny," said Hoddy.

"He was generous," Meade said hotly and paused. Hoddy's words struck her as if he had touched to life a spark somewhere in her consciousness. But then, what nonsense, she told herself. Sam must have been interested in every cause to which he contributed.

He must have been interested in her! He could have chosen any girl he wanted, but he had chosen little Meade Forrest, whom he had known since she was a long-legged child in carefully frayed and faded blue jeans and with her hair in her eyes. She had grown out of that phase by the time he returned to Havlock Place, the summer Andy left and the summer her father died. She was a young lady then and in complete reversal to her childish stages; now her hair was always shining and smooth, her dresses were properly crisp and clean; she even had one party dress, a frilly white cotton which she had worn when he asked her to marry him. He had come to call for her in the cottage, where her father's big desk chair was too empty and her Aunt Chrissy too tearful and talkative; so she had put on her white dress and he had taken her out along the road to the Sound and asked her to marry him, as casually as he had asked the boy at the filling station for gasoline.

So she said yes. Naturally. She must have meant it, although at the time it didn't seem quite real. There was no one to consult but Aunt Chrissy, and she knew what Aunt Chrissy would say—which she did when she told her that night of their engagement: "Oh, you lucky girl! You've made an old woman very happy." Then, suddenly, all the plans were made; it had to be a big wedding; Sam was a prominent person. There were discussions in which Meade, hating herself for it and helpless, pretended to take an interest. She didn't know then, and in her lost and forsaken state of mind, didn't realize that that particular pretense would go on and on and on. Yet if Sam found anything lacking in her attitude, he never gave any hint of it.

It struck her very early in her marriage how difficult it was for her to understand him—if, indeed, she ever did—but he was always kind.

They had decided on a long cruise on a commercial steamer, every luxury anybody could think of. In the main it had been a successful honeymoon, she supposed. She had thought too much of Andy; perhaps Sam had guessed that. Nevertheless, she knew they presented to the world an almost ideal picture of a newly married couple, with Sam showering her with gifts everywhere they went. Clothes, too, and jewels—heavens, the jewels, which were safely returned to some bank after an important occasion. "It's like asking to get bumped on the head to wear them," Sam had explained.

Hoddy said, "Here comes Brice. Tell him everything, Meade. If things don't go well, you're going to need a lawyer, aside from the Bacon outfit. I mean, just for you. Don't look so scared, he'll explain..."

Meade said stiffly, trying to control the sudden thuds of her heart, "The only thing that requires explanation is how Sam could have fallen from the terrace without being seen by anybody."

"Mr. and Mrs. Garnet," John announced in a lugubrious way. He had resumed his role as butler, but it was a butler who might have been employed by Lady Macbeth in one of her less cheery moods.

"Have the police really gone?" Hoddy asked.

John nodded. "Yes, sir," he all but moaned and went away.

"What's the matter with that guy?" Hoddy said sharply. "He looks as if he had a load on his conscience. That or he's afraid."

Agnes Garnet came in and put her arms for a moment around Meade, who had risen. Brice took her hand comfortingly, but his gray eyes were troubled. "I've just had a talk with Mr. Bacon. I

51

met him at the gate as he was leaving. He said he had explained some of Sam's affairs to you."

"Yes."

Agnes took a cigarette from the green jade box on Sam's magnificent mahogany desk; Sam, who never smoked himself, had always remembered that his guests might wish to, and the box was always filled with fresh cigarettes.

With a nervous jerk Hoddy leaned forward to light Agnes' cigarette, but she had already done so. Her light hair was satin-smooth; her pink-and-white candy-striped dress was neat and cool-looking; her slim legs were bare and tanned. A huge emerald shone on her right hand; only her wedding ring was on her left hand. Meade knew that Agnes was happy with her marriage and her two children, Peter and Anne, now at summer camp. Agnes adored them both; Brice tried unsuccessfully to conceal his own paternal pride.

Brice sat down, frowning a little. "Now then, I don't really know how to say this, Meade, so I'll just say it. I understand the police were here this morning, too. Why?"

"They said Sam's accident was unusual. Chief Haggerty said—I don't remember just how he put it..."

"Anything unusual struck him as something he ought to investigate," Hoddy prompted her. "Not those exact words, but that was the idea."

"I can understand that. It *was* very strange. The medical man says there was no indication of heart failure, nothing that could have caused a blackout or—oh, something of the kind. We'll have more exact reports later, after the laboratory—well, well..." He seemed to be trying to save Meade's feelings. "We'll have to wait for a final assessment of his death—an official verdict of accident, I mean. Now, this Mr. Bacon spoke of Sam's money."

"Yes."

Agnes said in her cool, pleasant voice, "According to Mr. Bacon, you will be a very rich woman, Meade."

Meade shook her head. "I can't take it in. Oh, I knew Sam had money, but I never dreamed it was so—so much."

Brice nodded. "That was like Sam. Never wanted to throw his weight around. Always in the background. Mr. Bacon says he, or one of his firm, drew up Sam's will. It is an excellent firm. You can't do better than to leave all business affairs in their hands. They'll investigate everything, don't worry about that. All this will take time. Did Sam ever tell you about any notes or letters or anything concerning his financial affairs here in the house?"

"I don't think so. We never talked of his business interests. No, I'm sure he never brought business letters or notes from his New York office."

Agnes glanced around the luxurious room. "Not even a safe," she said soberly.

"No," Meade replied, although at the same time, way back in her consciousness there was a kind of tinkle, as if she knew something that she didn't really know and yet it was associated with a faint aura of amusement. She tried to fish out that fugitive memory, if that was what it was, but failed, and then John came softly into the room to ask if Mr. and Mrs. Garnet would be there for lunch, which he did in a secretive and worried manner in Meade's ear—quite as if Lady Macbeth were lurking nearby in an impatient frame of mind. Agnes said no, they had to go home.

John nodded, sighed and left. Brice looked after him. "If that fellow hasn't got a prison record somewhere, I'll eat my hat."

Hoddy said suddenly, "If things—I mean, if somebody in some little lab comes out with something like, say, like poison..."

Brice's gaze sharpened. "What makes you think that, my boy?"

"The way they act. Haggerty keeps saying there's something he doesn't understand. I should think they'd just agree it was an accident. What else could it have been?"

Brice said, frowning, "I suppose it could have been poison. But I don't see how he could have been poisoned. He seemed perfectly normal when he picked up his drink and dropped ice into it. I took some ice, too. I do remember that clearly. Agnes likes just a taste of your aunt's Southern Comfort, so I poured that for her. After that I don't remember anything special until Meade came up the steps and all at once somebody said, 'Where is Sam?'"

"Aunt Chrissy," said Hoddy.

"Yes. We all know what happened after that, and it really is unusual. I can understand Haggerty's feeling that he wants to get it all straight in his head. Got a bit of a thick head, Haggerty; however, he's a good man. But, Meade, if anything goes wrong—it's a pity Andy came back just when he did. Did you by any chance see or talk to Andy at any time before the—accident?"

They were all hesitating now before the use of the word "accident." Meade said, "Yes. Chief Haggerty knows that. Andy had a game of tennis with Hoddy. I went down and talked a little while with him and then he went away. He came back here after his cousin Isabel had seen the police cars and all that. You were here. You spoke to him."

"Yes, of course, but did anybody see you talking to him down at the tennis court?"

"Yes. John saw us. He told Chief Haggerty."

Brice thought that over and sighed. "Too bad. Everybody knows that you were engaged to him and then suddenly he went away and you married Sam."

54

Very distantly, probably from the pantry, there was the sound of a telephone ringing; Sam would never permit a phone in his magnificent study.

Meade half heard the phone. She said, "It was perfectly natural for me to see Andy. Hoddy told me that he was here, down at the tennis court. An old friend. There was no possible reason why I shouldn't see him."

But of course there was every reason. It seemed to her that Brice's keen eyes read her thoughts. But at that moment John opened the door—and a John who had been informed that Lady Macbeth had definitely placed him next on her list of casualties. "Madam, he was murdered! He was poisoned. They said so. Poison!"

Four

Brice's face tightened; Agnes put out her half-smoked cigarette and then lighted another with shaking hands. There was at the same time a kind of scramble and thud as Hoddy started forward, tripped over a footstool and then fell flat.

Brice said tensely, "*Who* said he was poisoned?"

John gulped. "The police. The chief. They got the report from some laboratory. Mr. Havlock was poisoned."

"But how—" Brice began and stopped abruptly.

Agnes went to Hoddy, knelt down and put her hand on his pulse. "He seems to be unconscious. I hope he's not badly hurt."

This roused Hoddy, who struggled to get up and said indignantly, "I'm not hurt at all. I just bumped my head. Did John really say that Sam was poisoned?"

"He did," Brice said shortly. "Get up on your feet, boy. John, bring in some brandy. I think Mrs. Havlock could do with some."

Meade was sitting back in her chair, leaning far back because she felt peculiarly dizzy. She eyed her hand lying on the armrest as if she'd never seen it before. It was her left hand, with its plain wedding ring, which Sam had liked, and the enormous diamond, which he had also liked. Contradictions, perhaps. Sam couldn't have been poisoned.

She struggled to get out words. "But he was there...on the terrace...with all of you. He fell..."

"Who gave him his drink?" Hoddy said, sitting up.

Brice glanced at him. "He just picked it up. I told you. I saw him. Drink was already mixed for him."

"Oh, my God," said Hoddy in a choked voice, staring at Meade.

Brice followed his gaze, slapped his forehead and cried out, for once in tune with Hoddy, "I'd forgotten! We used to joke about it. Sam always said she made his special drink better than any bartender." He took a long breath. "By any chance, Meade—I mean, you *were* down at the tennis court talking to Andrew Brooke. By any chance, did you forget to mix that drink for Sam?"

Hoddy stared at the floor. Meade said, "No, I mixed it just as usual. Then I put a paper napkin over it. It's the way we always did. Sam always said nobody else could mix it to suit him."

"And it was a lot of junk," Hoddy said dully.

"That doesn't mean there was poison in it," Agnes said sharply. "Do pull yourselves together. You're acting as if the police will automatically say that Meade added a spoonful of arsenic to his drink."

"He'd never have known it with all that garbage," Hoddy began and in horror clapped his hand over his mouth.

Brice turned to John. "Did Haggerty tell you what *kind* of poison?"

John shook his head. "All he said was to tell Mrs. Havlock the results of the laboratory tests. And that he might not be able to see her until this evening. I gathered that there were investigations he wished to make concerning the poison."

"Did he say that in so many words?"

John reflected. "Honest, Mr. Garnet, I don't remember exactly what he said. Except that it was poison. All I could think of was that Florrie and I helped with the drinks. But I didn't poison the drink. I wouldn't think of it. Besides—"

"Besides, he was very good to you and Florrie and neither of you was at all likely to get another job in a hurry," Hoddy said. "Nobody blames you, John. You had no reason for killing the goose—oh, Lord, I mean hurting your benefactor."

A faint look of relief came into John's pallid face. "No, sir."

But Meade thought numbly, I mixed that drink. All of them know it.

Everybody knew that she had seen Andy; everybody knew or soon would know about the money Sam's death would bring her. Unless, of course (impossible, a nightmare), a jury found her guilty of murder. Then she couldn't inherit anything at all. That was the law and Hoddy had remembered it.

There was a thick kind of silence in the room; suddenly Meade realized that no one was looking at her, yet she was so clearly the focus of their thoughts that she might as well have been put on a pedestal and stared at. She felt guilty, almost as if she were in fact guilty.

The door opened and Andrew Brooke came in.

Brice roused sharply. "Andy, you shouldn't have come!"

"I had to," Andy said, looking at Meade.

"You'll be of more help to Meade if you'll stay

59

away from this place. Here in the Cove everybody knows everybody else's business. So stay away."

"I saw the police car leaving," Andy said quietly. "Have they made any progress?"

"The police say it was poison," Meade said dully.

"Poison! It can't be . . ." Andy was suddenly very white.

"That's what they say," Brice said and added, appealing, "*Please* listen to me, Andy. *Stay away.*"

Hoddy suddenly perked up. "They acted very suspicious, *I* think. In any event, what comes next, Brice?"

Brice rubbed his graying thick hair. "Well, first they'll gather what evidence they can. Identify the poison. Try to find out who could have got hold of it and where. Yes, that would be the logical course. Then a hearing, which in our county means that the judge listens to all the evidence. It's not a trial; it has neither a prosecutor nor a defense lawyer; no questions except to ask any witnesses to tell what they saw of the event. But this may not be called for some time."

"Why not?" Andy asked.

"It's been a while since I functioned in court." Brice rubbed his hair again. "In this county the calendar is always crowded. Also, as a rule the important witnesses are in such an emotional state just after the—tragedy occurs that they are likely to make inaccurate statements. If enough time is given them to cool down, their statements are likely to be far more accurate. I suppose that's why the medical examiner made such copious notes last night."

"I didn't notice that," Hoddy said.

"I did. He wanted to have all the details down on paper so no questions would trip him up later. Safer for him to make notes immediately than to try to remember these details. Oh, it's the custom
60

and a good one. But if eventually the judge decides that the evidence strongly suggests that any one person poisoned Sam, then that person will be incarcerated." He carefully avoided looking at Meade. "Then the whole problem goes to the state's attorney, an indictment and—well, later, a trial. Oh, never mind all this. It is a lengthy process. Bail may be set, in this instance very high bail. If it's accepted, the person under indictment may be freed pending a trial. There is some variation of the process, depending largely upon the opinions of the judge and the State's attorney. Nothing can be done now. Agnes—"

Florrie stuck her head in the door. "Cold lunch on the terrace," she announced flatly and disappeared.

Brice's astute lawyer's face tightened. "Why on earth should Sam choose to pick out a couple of out-of-work actors and bring them right into the house!"

"I'll tell you why." Agnes's voice was suddenly very clear. "You go to an employment agency yourself, Brice. Tell them just what you want—cook, housemaid, gardener, anything—and see what you get. See what you *don't* get is more like it. And if anybody turns up, it's to interview you, not for you to interview him. You don't know what I've gone through just to keep our little house going."

"But with all Sam's money! Good heavens, *some* people manage to get good servants. Why didn't Sam? He must have plenty of flunkies around for office work when he's away traveling or something. Why couldn't they try to find regular servants for him?"

"But Sam wanted these people," Agnes said. "And if it amused him to hire them, it's none of our business, is it?"

Brice's eyes were very thoughtful. "I still wonder about those Elwells. Maybe there was some special reason Sam employed them ..."

"Now, Brice," Agnes said sharply, "I wouldn't hint at dark secrets about Florrie and John. Believe me, they are just what they seem. They had no hold over Sam."

"If they had had," Hoddy muttered, "I told you, I told them: they wouldn't have killed the goose—"

Brice broke in, "I don't care for them and that's a fact. Even the idea seems—oh, impulsive. Yet Sam could do just such impulsive things, at least when he was younger. Good heavens, I've known him forever. Of course, as he grew older he became more and more conventional."

"Sam was always conventional," Meade cried, astonished.

Brice smiled at her. "Not when we were in school together. That is, Sam was much younger. I was about to graduate from law school." Turning to his wife, he said, "We'd better go, Agnes."

Brice and Agnes had left when Hoddy said, "May as well eat," and led the way to the terrace, the same terrace where they had talked the night before and from which Sam had gone down to his death. Aunt Chrissy adjusted her eyeglasses, went over to look down at the slope and said, "I always thought this balustrade was too low. A man of Sam's size—dear, dear!"

Hoddy helped himself lavishly to cold meat and a rather peculiar-looking salad, then thought of Meade and handed the plate to her. "Chivalry?" Andy said rather sharply. "Really, Hoddy, do you think Meade can get away with all that mess?"

"I'll make myself a sandwich." Meade reached for some bread when Aunt Chrissy cried sharply, "What's that?"

All three ran to look over the balustrade. Aunt Chrissy was pointing, her manicured white hand shaking. "It looks like ... it's red and ... I declare, it looks like one of those maraschino cherries Sam always liked in that horrible drink of his."

It was undoubtedly one of the cherries, round and glistening in the sunlight.

Andy, the first to pull himself together, went for the phone.

"Where are you going?" Hoddy asked. "What for?"

"The police couldn't have searched the place thoroughly enough last night. They missed that."

"Oh!" Hoddy grew almost solemn. "And it might have some of the poison in it that they say Sam—" He scrambled after Andy. Aunt Chrissy remained, giving as good an impersonation of a bird dog pointing as a very stately woman could give. "Right there it is! Don't take your eyes off it, Meade. They missed it last night! It wouldn't show up like that in the dark." She leaned far over the balustrade. "It *is* steep, isn't it? I never realized how steep. But with all those pines and shrubbery and things, you'd have thought that Sam could have caught hold of one. Unless he was completely unconscious. And I don't see how—"

"All right, Aunt Chrissy! We know where the cherry is. The police will find it. Please come away. There's lunch waiting, you know."

"Oh well, yes." Aunt Chrissy was always interested, in a dignified manner, but interested, in her meals. She munched her way solidly through quite a quantity of food. "If you can call this salad lunch," she said. "Honestly, Meade, you've got to get rid of those down-at-the-heels actors. Why, it wouldn't surprise me one bit if Florrie or John poisoned him. They had a good chance, too."

"But he gave them employment. We've been all over that, Aunt Chrissy."

"You can't be sure," Aunt Chrissy said darkly. "If I were Haggerty, I'd look into the past of those two." She nibbled a lettuce leaf rather in the fashion of a suspicious but aristocratic rabbit and said, "Maybe they had a hold on Sam. One reads of

63

those things. Revenge for long-past deeds."

"Aunt Chrissy, can you really imagine Sam doing anything that would provoke revenge from anyone in the world?"

She swallowed her lettuce leaf. "Frankly, no, I can't. He was too careful not to step on anybody's toes. Seems too bad, though. They've got to find a murderer and I'd rather it were Florrie or John."

So would I, Meade thought in spite of herself, because then she herself—or possibly Andy, nobody else could be suspected of murder. But it could still be some odd kind of accident. Couldn't it?

Before Meade had poured coffee, the steep rugged slope down to the Sound was crawling with policemen, blue uniforms everywhere, Haggerty surveying and directing, while the others combed the bushes and rocks. Aunt Chrissy strolled majestically across the terrace to watch as soon as she heard the commotion; Meade followed. She saw Chief Haggerty put the small red cherry very carefully in a cellophane envelope. He then disappeared.

After a while Andy and Hoddy returned to the house, hot and tired. "Haggerty says if the poison was in Sam's drink, it'll show in the cherry," Andy told Meade. "It seems the lab boys are sure it was poison. I don't know how they know so much, something about muscular reaction or nonreaction or—oh, never mind that, but it wasn't any of the usual poisons like, say, arsenic or cyanide. So perhaps the cherry, if it was soaked in it, will give them the information they want."

"And I put two cherries in his drink," Meade said miserably.

Andy's eyes flashed. "You took them out of a bottle, didn't you? Meade, show some sense. We all know you didn't poison Sam. Now then, just in case," Andy said hurriedly, "get a lawyer to look out for you. Say, Brice."

"He's running for governor," Meade said dismally. "Sam made the nominating speech. Brice has got to cover the state making speeches, getting votes, all that before the first Tuesday in November. They toured the state last spring, Brice and Sam, too, as a rule, but now Brice must get in the hard work. He simply can't take time out for me."

Aunt Chrissy said thoughtfully, "It would put Brice in a difficult position, of course. If it comes to a—we have to face it, a trial—"

Meade thought, The world cannot be like this; nothing is substantial.

Aunt Chrissy went on, showing one of her hidden talents for acumen, much as Hoddy did, "If it should come to a trial and Brice defended you successfully, he'd damn himself."

Andy's eyes were like flints. "Why do you say that?"

"Perfectly obvious. If he gets Meade off, people will say it's because of the money she'll inherit. Hoddy told me. *Three hundred million dollars*— dear me! People will say that Brice was bribed; they'll say naturally a girl with so much money wouldn't be found guilty of anything. But if he *doesn't* get her off, he'll go straight to the governor's mansion. Everybody will say he's an honest man; they'll say he refused to be bribed." Aunt Chrissy dusted a crumb from her delicate rose-sprigged dress. "Meade's conviction will send him to the governor's chair. Her acquittal will damn him forever as far as public office goes."

Hoddy gave a sigh like a groan.

Meade said, "He can't take the chance..."

There was a rustle at the door. Florrie, still in the rather soiled and certainly flashy dress she had donned that morning instead of her "French-maid role" uniform, did have the grace to announce grumpily that Mrs. Garnet had come back.

Agnes managed to give Florrie a look which would have frozen most women in their tracks but bounced off Florrie. Then she came forward and took Meade's hands. "Brice and I have been thinking it over. He thinks you might be arrested, Meade darling. If so, he will act as your lawyer. That is, if you want him."

"If I want him!" Meade cried and then checked herself. "But, Agnes, if"—she forced herself to say it—"if I'm arrested and indicted, or whatever they do, and sent to trial and Brice defends me and gets me off—"

"There, now," Agnes said swiftly, "we've talked over all of that. Brice says right is right. He does not believe you murdered Sam and therefore he does not believe that any evidence can be brought out to prove you guilty."

"But if he gets me off—"

"You're thinking that the voters will say: 'Rich girl.' They'll speculate about how much bribe money was paid and to whom—public prosecutors, even the jury, especially your lawyer's fee. They'll say, 'One law for the rich, another for the poor.' But, my dear child, *you didn't kill Sam!* Brice says people will recognize the facts and will be far more likely to vote for somebody who stuck to his friends, in spite of everything, until the truth could be established, than if he—"

"—washed his hands of the whole affair," Aunt Chrissy concluded.

"He is perfectly sure that Meade's complete innocence can be established," Agnes went on. "But he says it's very early yet. Good heavens, this happened only last night. Now, this cherry they've found..."

Andy said, "How did you know about that?"

Agnes turned her calm, half-smiling look at him. "Dear Andy, you've been away too long. You've forgotten how news travels at the Cove. As a matter of fact, the grocery boy told me just as I was leaving the house. And while I think of it, Andy"—her face became extremely earnest—"I wouldn't stay around here, I mean around Meade and the Havlock place. Everybody remembers your romance with Meade before she married Sam. Brice is right. They'll say—"

Florrie came to the door, eying Meade with a kind of covert impudence. "The chief of police asked me for the open bottle of cherries, the one you took the cherries from last night. And then he wanted the bottle of bitters, and then he took away the sugar bowl we keep on the bar."

"That's all right," Meade said.

But Florrie lingered. "I just want to say, Madam"—she underlined the "Madam" in an almost insulting way—"John and I are leaving. We don't intend to work where there's been a murder."

"Oh yes, you will." A gleam of triumph came into Agnes' face. "The police will not let you leave."

Florrie's smug expression faded a little. "Oh," she said after some thought and departed.

"Good gracious," Meade said, "I didn't realize she hated me so much."

"Jealous," Agnes said. "You had everything. Natural in a way, especially for a nature like Florrie's. Too bad you couldn't just kick her out bodily. Hoddy and Andy would do it for you."

"No," Andy said soberly. "If Haggerty wants them to stay, they'll have to stay."

"Well, yes. Good-bye now, Meade. Don't worry. There's simply no evidence against you. Brice said that."

"No evidence," Aunt Chrissy murmured dourly to herself, "except a returned lover, poison in a drink Meade mixed and three hundred million dollars."

Five

Again that had a stunning, numbing effect. Meade literally could not speak.

"I've lived a long time." Aunt Chrissy smoothed back her neat white hair. "You wouldn't believe the things I've seen. Or suspected."

Hoddy was angry. He went to his aunt and grasped her straight shoulders. "You can just shut up! Another word like that out of you, Aunt Chrissy, and I—I—"

"Hoddy, dear boy," his aunt said, unperturbed, "you mustn't get upset like that, right after eating, too. I'm going upstairs to rest. I advise you to do the same, Meade. As for you, Andy, inhospitable though it does seem, I feel that you should cease your visits here. You do understand, don't you, dear boy?" With which Aunt Chrissy departed in her usual stately manner.

Andy leaned back in his chair and looked at the shabby sneakers he was wearing. Hoddy muttered under his breath something to the effect that Aunt Chrissy was a meddlesome old fool.

Andy rose. "She tells the truth, though. I'm going into town. Maybe there's some news somewhere. Coming, Hoddy?"

Hoddy jumped at the thought of action of any kind.

That afternoon Meade had an unexpected interview with Mrs. Dunham. It was better to move than just sit and think of all the possibilities that might develop; she went down the steps to the bench on the landing and the rarely used flight of steps going down almost to the water. From there she could see the blue-clad men (although when she counted, there were only four of them) still searching through the sparse shrubbery; once or twice Sam had murmured something about doing that slope in proper style with attractive planting. He had never done it. The men were of course searching for anything at all that was connected with Sam. Another cherry? A button? A scrap of material? Anything. She went on down the steps to the tennis court.

Perhaps now the house could be sold. Mr. Bacon and the other executors might see to that and other domestic matters and payrolls; there was the huge and very luxurious apartment in New York, where full housekeeping services, perfect room service, good china, good silver, good crystal were all supplied. She had wondered how much the entire arrangement must have cost, but since it obviously hadn't bothered Sam, she had never asked him. He really did not like to talk of money; his interviews with his business associates—the quiet, reserved men with the quiet, reserved faces and neat briefcases tucked under their quiet, reserved and well-tailored arms—were, now that she thought of it, a little unwelcome to Sam. He was always glad to see them go and would come to her and suggest, if it was nearing dusk, that she make him what he called his Havlock Special.

His Havlock Special was simply a notion he had taken; she thought it entertained him to watch her put together such a surprising drink. "Shocking," one of their infrequent guests had called it, a look of horror on his face. But she had discovered over those three years that the fact was that Sam had virtually no sense of taste; it was like having no sense of hearing or no sense of smell. He never mentioned it; even when she spoke of it he merely smiled but once told her it was laughable to see the faces of his guests when he drank, without tasting it at all, the Havlock Special. Childish of him, he had said. As indeed it was, but it amused him.

Well, now one of the cherries was—where? In some laboratory being tested for this or that poison.

She was vaguely surprised to note that the afternoon was well advanced. The morning with its long interviews, its many visitors, luncheon with its own events had drawn on time. It didn't seem possible, but already the shadows under the pines were growing long and the sky had its sunset tinge of lemon and pink. She hadn't seen the dogs all day.

During the many times when she accompanied Sam on his trips, lately around the state to make his speeches about civic affairs, the local vet, Waldo Smith, had come to see that the dogs were fed, watered, exercised, and the kennels kept clean. When she was at home, she had seen to it herself that the dogs were taken care of with, when needed, the advice of Dr. Smith, who was a dedicated veterinarian and the cause of Meade's acquiring what Hoddy called her menagerie. Actually, there were only three dogs and it was mere chance that they were all Kerry blue terriers.

How kind, if rather impatient, Sam had been!

71

Her first Kerry blue, Marcelline, had just been a dog wandering across the road, having escaped the vet's pen, when the car Meade was driving swerved to avoid her, but not widely enough. She stopped and hurried to the injured puppy, although Sam was already late to some meeting. "She can't be hurt much," Sam said. "Come on, Meade. We'll be late."

But she had scooped up the puppy and turned to meet the veterinarian; young Dr. Smith, whom she came later and quickly to know as Waldo. His face was narrow and very thin; he had a sharp, big nose, narrow cheekbones and a tiny mouth and chin. He came hustling from his office, his white coat rumpled, and picked up the puppy, who instantly recovered. Marcelline gave Meade a long look through thick black hair which had not yet been clipped, wriggled so hard that Waldo put her down, and then trotted unsteadily to Meade and permitted Meade to take her up in her arms.

"She likes you," Waldo said in a high, squeaky voice, but smiling fondly. "That's something in a Kerry blue! Takes them a long time as a rule to put up with anybody at all. But very fine watchdogs," he added hurriedly, promoting a possible sale.

Marcelline snuggled a very black, cold nose into Meade's neck. Meade had the sense to ask her age.

"Just nine months ... If you were thinking of buying—that is, she can be ... altered when she's a little over a year, say. I wouldn't advise it sooner. That is, of course, if you were thinking of buying her."

Sam, looking at his watch, cut Waldo short, asked the price, paid the first sum mentioned, and told Waldo he could mail the pedigree papers later on.

But the altering of Marcelline came too late. "A very smart little bitch," Waldo had said, eying her first litter, one wriggling little male. "Now, as soon as she has finished nursing him—" But Marcelline

72

had been too smart and presented another puppy in almost record time.

There was a bit of discussion as to how Marcelline had contrived her romances, but Waldo was sure that she had simply found her way back to his kennels and one of his own fine Kerry blues.

The two puppies proved to be fine, but ferocious when they felt in any way disparaged. For the safety of chance callers, and also to curb Marcelline's passion for unbridled motherhood (now bridled surgically but not emotionally), Sam had kennels built, strongly fenced, with all the suitable arrangements for feeding and watering, and even a small room for trimming and bathing.

It was another example of Sam's generosity to her; he didn't really like dogs.

Turning the corner of the vine-laden fence, Meade saw the figure of a woman dressed in black sitting on the bench just outside the kennels. All three dogs were nudging at the wire. It was Mrs. Dunham who had been in the habit of taking down scraps from the kitchen to feed them; Meade had forbidden it, explaining the diet Waldo had prescribed. Mrs. Dunham had merely replied that she knew as much and more about dogs than Waldo Smith, and her cooking was such that Meade did not have the courage to defy her. She had been thankful for Mrs. Dunham's cooking, but she had never felt at ease with the stern woman who sat composed on the bench, watching with bright, knowing black eyes.

"I thought you'd come down here sooner or later," Mrs. Dunham said. "I want to talk to you."

"All right," Meade said after a moment's pause, for she certainly didn't want to talk to Mrs. Dunham, who was probably about to give notice. She was not the stereotyped image of a fine cook. She was thin, not plump; sour, not good-natured. She was cross and hard to please; she also had a rigorously accurate idea of the times they lived in. She would work only certain hours, only time to shop for and prepare dinner, but a superb dinner, which she left for Florrie and John to serve. Then she drove away, superbly too, in her shiny new car.

She said now, "I thought I'd better tell you. I was on that little terrace up there above the tennis court when you met young Andrew Brooke. I saw and heard everything."

So Hoddy really had seen someone, barely a glimpse. Meade's heart began to thud.

Mrs. Dunham's black eyes were vigilant. "That bothers you? Well, it ought to. Talk of divorce! All that money! And your husband died that very night of poison from a drink you mixed for him." She leaned forward. "What man wouldn't want some of that wealth? Maybe you two together planned Mr. Havlock's murder. A girl Andrew Brooke once wanted but then doesn't want until she is very rich. And if her husband doesn't want a divorce, as anyone would say and young Brooke must have guessed, then take the shortcut. Poison his drink. Wife gets all his money. It's what people will say. Probably be right. If they knew all this, of course. I expected you might have seen me watching you and Mr. Brooke and perhaps wanted to talk to me privately. Have you decided?"

"Decided?"

"Decided how much to pay me," Mrs. Dunham said impatiently.

"Pay?"

"For most people—yes, I think I can say, for everybody—I can judge the amounts pretty accurately. For you, I'm not so sure. A boy at the filling station said he'd heard it was three hundred million. H'm," Mrs. Dunham said thoughtfully, "I expect a million would be about the right sum for me. Perhaps more."

Meade gasped. "Why, do you—you can't mean that you're involved in a—a business that's nothing short of blackmail!"

74

Mrs. Dunham chuckled. "A good business! Oh, I can't say I was surprised about this. Somebody—Florrie, I think—said that a young man was playing tennis with your brother and I remembered that somebody had said young Andrew Brooke was home, so I—call it put two and two together. And it certainly was worth seeing." She gave another vulturine chuckle. "All I did was slip back in a corner of the terrace so you couldn't see me, but I could hear you. All that talk about a divorce! And then—then all at once Mr. Havlock murdered in that dreadful way. How often I've seen him sitting there in his favorite place, looking up and down the Sound. You see for yourself, one in my business—"

"Business! Blackmail a business!"

"Don't talk so much. I was about to say that the amount of money—"

"Stop it!" Meade cried in a choked voice.

Something in her voice communicated with the dogs; they thrust up alert ears, all three of them suddenly stood very, very still and a kind of purple tinge came into their concerted gaze. Mrs. Dunham saw it; she rose abruptly. "Not that they would do anything to me—would you, my pretties?" she said, at which, to Meade's sudden clutch of almost hysterical glee, all three dogs set up a clamor of fury.

"I'll let the dogs out." Meade advanced toward the kennels, but Mrs. Dunham knew when enough was enough.

"I'll go now!" she cried. "Never mind opening the gate." She scuttled halfway down the gravel path toward the driveway, turned and called back, "Think over the amount. You can pay up or else..." She disappeared, swift as a black rat, toward her shining Mercedes, parked somewhere in the driveway.

Meade sat down limply on the bench. What a genius Mrs. Dunham had for blackmail, or rather what a genius she had displayed in thinking out her plan and carrying it through. She had certainly taken pains to become such a fine cook that to get one of Mrs. Dunham's meals was almost an inducement to accept anybody's invitation. Lately even Agnes had borrowed her expert services for an occasional bit of important political entertaining at the Garnet home. Her opportunities for digging out secrets had to be unlimited. But she must have kept her clients to a small list and, Meade realized with horror, a rich list. If she ever happened into a house where there were no secrets to dig out, Meade hadn't a doubt that Mrs. Dunham would leave, but not before she had secured a fine reference from her employer. Meade herself would have said without hesitation that Mrs. Dunham was a fine cook; that she was honest to the penny—and she had been, to the penny, but not when it came to thousands; hadn't she mentioned a million—that she did not drink; that she was reliable. She must look for Mrs. Dunham's references and turn the names over to—well, not to the police, but she must find out what her previous employers had known or would admit knowing.

What a background for high and fancy blackmail! "Servants know everything that happens in a house," her father had once said whimsically. "So perhaps it's just as well that we are financially obliged to have recourse to what our British cousins call a 'daily.' Or is it 'a char'? In any event, all our dark secrets can safely remain our own." There hadn't been any dark secrets, although there had been a good and faithful "daily."

The opportunities Mrs. Dunham had disclosed were stunning. And the point was that Mrs. Dunham intended to carry out her declared course. Pay up or else. Newspaper headlines leaped into Meade's mind.

She waited awhile, going into the pen, talking to the dogs, fussing over them until their eyes were dark and loving and they pushed against her knees with their customary affection.

It was by then definitely darker. Meade wondered whether Florrie and John were still around to perform their usual duties. Oddly enough, she was reasonably sure that Mrs. Dunham had prepared a superb dinner before she made her declaration. One thing she was entirely sure of, she hadn't seen the last of Mrs. Dunham.

At last she shoved the dogs gently away and closed the kennel gate. Loose, they had two courses; if the big driveway gate was open, they made a beeline for that and thence Marcelline headed for Waldo's place; if the driveway gate was closed, they seemed to know it and took a different route, across the tennis court, up the steps and onto the terrace, where Meade in an abandoned moment had once left a box of dog biscuits. Having done this once, they all but forced her to continue the delectable custom.

As she turned from them Florrie appeared, in proper uniform and white apron this time, her sullen face a little subdued. "They're waiting for you on the terrace," she said and added "Madam" as if it hurt.

"All right, Florrie. We'll have dinner there tonight. There'll only be two of us."

"Oh no..." Again Florrie contrived to sound impertinent as she said, "Oh no, Madam, there'll be you and your brother and Mr. Brooke and Mrs. Chrissy, of course, and Mr. and Mrs. Garnet. That's what your brother told me."

"We'll have dinner there, just the same. Where is John?"

"He's in bed. Says he has the chills."

Scared, Meade thought, but why? On the other hand, why not? Everybody in the house the previous night must feel uneasy. "We'll make it a buffet. We'll help ourselves, use the little glass-topped tables. I suppose Mrs. Dunham fixed dinner."

"Oh yes. She said that everything considered,

she thought it likely a buffet meal would be best."

Smart, far-seeing and evil Mrs. Dunham.

Florrie disappeared around a clump of shrubbery and Meade took her way across the tennis court, remembering too well the scene of the night before. The lemon-and-pink sky and the black shapes of shrubbery again etched themselves deeply as the sun fell.

She went slowly up the steps, glancing out over the waters of the Sound, quiet, pale in the middle, shadowed at the edges. This time she didn't stop at the bench, and when she looked over toward the slope where Sam had fallen, she saw that the blue-clad searchers were gone.

Agnes, Brice, Hoddy, Aunt Chrissy and Andy were waiting for her. They were actually waiting as if, she thought swiftly, they had something to tell her. It was Brice who spoke. "It was in the cherry. They also found pieces of the glass he'd been drinking from. You had put two cherries in it and they found the second cherry too. They took pieces of the glass and cherries—oh, and the bottle of cherries from your own pantry—away to the lab. So now they know what the poison is."

"Well, no," Andy said suddenly. "That's the problem. They *don't* know what it is. They just know it exists; it hasn't even got a real name yet, only a number, and it killed Sam."

Six

Brice said, "Sit down, Meade. I'll try to explain. At least this is what Haggerty told us. Haggerty and the medical examiner. It's a new drug. That is, it is probably a very old drug, but only recently surgeons have begun to use it, experimenting a little more and more successfully."

"It relaxes the muscles," Hoddy interrupted. "Completely. In a few seconds. That's why Sam didn't make a move, didn't do anything, just slid down into the water and drowned."

Meade sank down in one of the big wicker chairs.

"Hoddy is right in a way," Brice went on. "Its use, however, has not been precisely defined. The surgeon who uses it takes great chances. It may relax the muscles of his patient almost instantly and very helpfully, with no bad effects. But there

79

was a case somewhere, I don't remember where..."

"England," Hoddy said. "The chief said so."

"Was it? Well, in any event, the patient died when he shouldn't have died. This drug was considered the cause because if it's given in too great a proportion, the lungs stop working—heart, lungs, every muscle in the body just stops. So it is a very dangerous drug to use. Its use is so new that the side effects are not known."

Aunt Chrissy tapped the balustrade sharply with her glass. "Then why does any doctor use it?"

Brice sighed. "It's empirical—I mean, the reason it is ever used. It works because it works. Sometimes. Makes surgery easier for both the patient and the surgeon. But it must be used under very minutely controlled conditions."

"You said it hasn't even got a name?"

"No. In a way it somewhat resembles curare. That's a South American—"

"I know," Aunt Chrissy snapped. "Comes from plants. Deadly poison."

"Not if properly used. It may become a great benefit. So may this stuff.—"

"Why hasn't it got a name?"

"It has a number only, so far. Number 3 dash 256—something like that. Eventually they'll give it some name, Latin-sounding probably, or such a conglomeration of syllabyles that only the medics and pharmacists know what it refers to. But at this point, number 3 and so on is sufficient identification to the few who know it."

"So Sam got a big dose of this stuff," Aunt Chrissy said, "and it paralyzed him. That's what you're trying to say. Just completely paralyzed him so fast that he couldn't speak, couldn't do anything, lost all control of muscles or thinking or speaking, just slid right down off the balustrade! Where could anybody buy this stuff? Just anywhere?"

80

"No." Brice sighed again patiently. "I'm trying to tell you. The big hospitals in New York won't use it until there are more definite and certain data concerning it. Some laboratories are working on it. There are a few drug-supply houses which carry small amounts. The police will try to check those out, and the laboratories, but it will take time and possibly they'll never find out who got hold of this particular amount."

"It does sound like curare," said Andy. He was sitting not far from Aunt Chrissy, his elbows on his knees, his face deeply thoughtful.

Brice nodded. "Exactly what I told you. The point is, all this investigation will take time. It may never be solved. But of course, the poison *was* in the cherries they found, so it must have been put in Sam's drink. The question that concerns us is who put it there. It couldn't have been done by accident."

It seemed to Meade that everyone looked away from her so pointedly that they might as well have singled her out and said, "You mixed the drink. You put the poisoned cherries in it."

Everyone but Andy; he shook his head slightly and gave her an encouraging little smile. "Accidents happen," he said gravely.

"Yes, yes. That's the way things stand now. They say since they have evidence—that is, arrangements for the services for Sam can now be made."

"Here's your supper," Florrie said from the doorway.

"No poison in it, I hope," Hoddy muttered, which drew an exasperated look from Brice.

But nothing could ever daunt Hoddy's appetite. He rushed over to the neatly laid table. Andy came to help him, and the two of them served up plates and handed them around, politely if very soberly on Andy's part, and politely but impatiently on Hoddy's part, who fell to with zest as soon as he

81

had persuaded Aunt Chrissy to put down her glass on a small table and make way for her plate.

The evening air was soft, the sky tranquil, the little rush of the tide coming in as soothing as it had been the night before, but nothing—oh, nothing, Meade thought, was the same.

Brice and Agnes got up to leave as soon as coffee had been served by the still-sullen Florrie. "Too bad you can't get rid of that woman right now," Agnes said as Florrie vanished carrying out trays and plates. "She's no good."

"Yes, I agree. But Agnes," Meade said, "I don't know *what* to do!"

"You're going to stay right here until the skies clear," Brice answered her. "Get Agnes to help you make a list of the people you want to attend the services for Sam. How about Thursday? That's day after tomorrow. Plenty of time. Better send telegrams to his business associates."

Meade nodded. Aunt Chrissy was heard to mumble that she didn't know any of Sam's friends.

Andy came over to Meade while the others were clustered around the door to the house. "Take it easy. There's bound to be an answer. Maybe I can—well, anyway, I love you. Remember that, if it does any good."

"Yes," said Meade on a long breath.

Agnes advised her to take one of the sleeping pills. Hoddy went down to close the gates and let the dogs out of the kennel. "Probably tear me limb from limb, but little you care," he said crossly to Meade, then softened, put his arm around her and kissed her cheek. "Keep your chin up."

"She's all right. I'll go with you and fend off your dogs," Andy said with pretended lightness.

Then they were all gone. The dogs must have dashed past Hoddy and Andy without even pausing to explore, because all at once Marcelline and her two pups came panting up the wrought-iron steps to the terrace. All three of them sat down and looked at Meade, believing thoroughly in the power of the canine eye.

"Oh, all right," she said on the verge of crying, gave each one the nightly allowance of one large dog biscuit from the box she kept on the terrace and went to bed.

After a while she heard Hoddy slamming the front door and taking the steps at his usual three at one leap. Then the house was very quiet. She ought to be able to sleep. She was limp with weariness; it was as if every nerve was worn thin.

Mrs. Dunham would intensify her threat of blackmail, she had no doubt. But the threat might prove ineffectual. The police already knew that she had met Andy at the tennis court; Haggerty might have surmised in his experienced and observant way that it could have been a more or less emotional meeting; he might even have guessed that Andy was determined on her getting a divorce from Sam. But he couldn't be sure. However, if a blackmailer once told his tale, then he lost his power! That reflection was slightly—but only slightly—cheering. Perhaps Mrs. Dunham wouldn't report on the scene at the tennis court yet.

Suddenly, out of the darkness, came the thought: three hundred million dollars.

The words might have been emblazoned in fire above Meade's head. It was dazzling; it was impossible; it was simply not to be imagined. And yet, in the three years of her marriage the professor's little girl from the Cove had, almost by osmosis, become accustomed to money, a great deal of money, spent everywhere by everybody Sam knew and consequently she became acquainted with. Some of them seemed fairly well known to Sam; she had never felt that she knew any of the women on really friendly or even intimate terms. She had grown adjusted to their talk, their appearances at odd intervals, here and there; she could remember names and make

83

suitable replies, yet most of them talked a different language: "Where do you order your clothes?" "Look at the bracelet Harry made for me"— meaning the famous jeweler Harry Winston. Meade had bitten her tongue; later, when she asked Sam, he seemed surprised at her ignorance. "Why, he designed that emerald necklace you are wearing!" There was bridge with shocking stakes. Meade played a sound game of bridge and Sam had never minded when she lost, which she rarely did, anyway. She and Aunt Chrissy, her father and Hoddy had often played bridge, so she had been reasonably safe on that ground. She didn't know the names of owners of the various yachts they encountered or the complicated customs in yacht basins. In fact, thinking back now, she realized that most of the people whom they saw much of were concerned exclusively with state political and philanthropic matters. Most of them wouldn't have cared if she wore fake jewelry and a bargain-counter dress as long as she behaved quietly and agreeably. She believed that Sam liked his own people more than the often times flashy groups with whom he seemed to have superficial but friendly associations. Certainly there was no civic undertaking in which he was not interested, and he never refused when it came to giving money.

But among them all, she knew Agnes and Brice best. Agnes especially was different. Agnes was real and sensible and dear to her. The Garnets actually lived in Blue Water Cove, in a pleasant but unpretentious house across town. Brice had had his own way to make and he had done it, successfully. Agnes, older than Meade, had been a most reliable and welcome friend.

Gradually Meade had become well adjusted— too well adjusted perhaps, she thought with a twinge of something like fear—to the use of a great deal of money. Still, three hundred million dollars

84

was a very, *very* great deal of money. Much could be done with it. She thought of Hoddy, set up in some serious career. Aunt Chrissy able to travel in luxury at all times. Sam would have wanted her to keep up his long list of charities.

Oh yes, unconsciously she had become accustomed to the luxury, the attentiveness of headwaiters or doormen, or anybody who might render Sam the slightest service. But she must be sensible about it—that is, if she was free to be sensible about anything! Don't think of murder, she told herself; don't think of being tried or possibly found guilty of murder. Don't think of that. Think of the responsibility of all that money.

Three hundred million dollars. Not three hundred thousand: she considered that; yes, she thought, given some sound advice, she could cope with that without throwing Sam's money away on trivial or even fraudulent causes.

Yet—Sam hadn't really loved her! Suddenly now in the middle of the night it seemed an utterly convincing truth; Sam had been generous, unfailing in his courtesy, but he hadn't been in love with her.

So why had he married her? Had another woman, somebody he truly loved, failed him? Had he felt that in his position he ought to have a wife, a wife whom he had known from childhood, whose background he was entirely familiar with and approved?

Perhaps she had failed him as a wife. Perhaps she had thought too much and too sadly of her break with Andy, and Sam had sensed that. Yet he had been a perfect if sometimes unpredictable husband—but not in love with her.

It was too late now to do anything but go through the formalities with all the dignity he would have demanded, and hope that she wouldn't be arrested and charged with his murder. That sent her huddling into the pllows.

Marcelline, out somewhere in the darkness, gave a small high-pitched yip. She and her offspring were magnificent watchdogs, of course. Nobody could enter the place while they were at large and roaming the grounds.

But someone did.

Stirring in her sleep, Meade thought that there was only a kind of stirring of air in her room as if the wind had come up.

Then she began to get a stronger impression. There *had* been some light sounds.

There *had* been the stirring of air in her room.

Suddenly she knew that there was a sound near her bedroom door. It had barely awakened her.

Aside from the little yip from Marcelline, hours ago perhaps, there had not been a sound from the dogs. So she was mistaken. No stranger could have come in without a hullabaloo from the dogs.

But someone had been near her. All at once she was wide awake and reaching for her bedside light.

The room was just the same. No difference; no difference except—why, yes, the door to the hall was ajar. The person trying to close it softly had apparently been so careful that there was only a slight motion and breath of air. She got out of bed, bewildered, not knowing what to do.

Then she knew—not what to do, but what had been done. A drawer of the Chinese Chippendale wall desk across the room was just slightly open. She never left a drawer open that way.

She had to look.

She went softly across the room. She had a feeling that someone was standing just outside her room in the hall, listening. She reached the drawer and very slowly, almost noiselessly, so the listener in the hall could not overhear, she pulled it out. Down in one corner stood a vial. She took it in her hand to examine it more closely. It was a small bottle; it would hold perhaps half an ounce or so.

On the red label were a skull and crossbones, and the word "Poison"; the label was torn, so the rest of whatever had been there was gone and only a faint smear of paper was left.

A dreadful thought flashed through her mind. She shouldn't have taken it in her hands. She shouldn't have put her fingerprints on it. She shouldn't have done that because someone was trying to cast a terrible suspicion on her. Frame her, that was the phrase—frame her for Sam's murder.

She was cold. The night breeze was mild but she was shivering. Call Hoddy. Call somebody. Even Aunt Chrissy.

First, look out in the hall, where there is a listener.

No, first put down the little bottle. Put it down anywhere. Hide it? No, no, first wipe off her own fingerprints. Fingerprints could be fatal. Fingerprints on an empty vial which was labeled "Poison" and could have held what they called only number something or other.

The hall door opened and a rush of cold air swept into the room. Meade whirled around, instinctively clutching the bottle behind her to hide it. A startling figure in swirling purple was standing in the doorway. The long purple garment ceased to be startling, for she recognized it as a robe Hoddy had brought back from Paris, saying that it satisfied his artistic instincts. He stared at her, his eyes puzzled yet seeing everything. "What have you got there? Meade, what in the world are you doing?"

"Who is in the hall?"

"In the—why, nobody." But he glanced over his shoulder. "That is, it's dark. But I did hear some sound. Like somebody running..."

"Turn on the hall lights! Hoddy, do as I say; don't stop to question!"

"Well, all right, but—"

"No. Wait. I'll get something." She ran into

Sam's bedroom, where he had kept his golf irons, and flung open the closet, filled with raincoats, caps, golf clubs. She hastily pulled out a club and ran back to Hoddy, who that time saw the bottle still clutched in her hand.

He grasped her wrist, looked at the bottle and said at last in a whisper, "Where'd you get that? That could be it. Couldn't it?"

"I don't know! It was there..." She showed him the drawer; she told in a whisper what had roused her; then she thought, But we're losing time! "Hurry, Hoddy—whoever put it there must have gotten into the house somehow. Hurry! Here, take the club."

"But if it is the murderer, I need a gun!"

"There is no gun."

"Oh yes, there is, and I know where Sam kept it. Them. A whole supply. I know how to get into the cabinet. Stay here. Now mind me. Don't move."

She couldn't move. She had to move. She had to get rid of that bottle. Yet it might be evidence which the police should have.

She couldn't hear Hoddy. He must have gone downstairs and into Sam's study. She remembered the beautifully carved cabinet against the wall. Hadn't Sam once said it was a gun rack? Hoddy must have known about it. Hoddy had almost a childlike fascination for exploring—prying she had called it once severely when catching him with unopened letters he was nosing through.

Now she was momentarily thankful for his nosiness and for the sharpness of his hearing.

But this bottle, what could she do with it? To hide it would only be to find no excuses when someone found it; no, that was dangerous. She hurriedly washed off every little scrap of the label until she held only a small clean bottle wrapped loosely in a handkerchief with no possible trace of its origin.

88

But she must hide it. What was Hoddy doing? She could hear nothing from below; she went into the hall, and there was Aunt Chrissy. "Whatever is the matter, Meade?" she asked. "I saw Hoddy downstairs and he had a *gun* in his hand! And what have you got there?"

Aunt Chrissy had eyes like a cat's.

"Did you hear anything in the hall a few minutes ago? Anything or ... or anybody?"

Aunt Chrissy's eyes widened. She put up a hand to smooth her already smooth hair; it was an example of one of Aunt Chrissy's classic pieces of advice: "Better to lose one's virtue than one's vanity." Not exactly appropriate the time she admonished a fourteen-year-old Meade about neat and careful grooming, but Meade's father had merely smiled when he heard it. It was a rule of Aunt Chrissy's life; even now, in the middle of the night, her hair was impeccable and she wore a delicate silk dressing gown edged with lace. But she was sharp enough, too. "What's that bottle in your hand?"

Aunt Chrissy, like Hoddy, was a born noser-out of secrets.

"It's an empty bottle! Aunt Chrissy, you shouldn't be wandering around the house like that. It's too cold."

"You've only got your nightgown on."

"I'm going back to bed. So are you, and—"

A single loud shot shattered the silence of the dark night outside the house.

The crashing sound seemed to linger in the stillness but there was nothing more, no shots, no running feet, no shouts, no voices of any kind. Strange—not a single dog set up a roar.

After a long, long moment, Aunt Chrissy said calmly, "Somebody's shooting at something."

Meade ran down the stairs. Aunt Chrissy followed.

The lights were all turned on, revealing only empty rooms and halls. So where was Hoddy?

The telephone rang so sharply and so unexpectedly that it shocked her almost as much as the gunshot. There was a tiny room beside a coat closet just below the stairs, large enough for a small chair and a telephone shelf. The phone rang again demandingly, so she picked up the receiver, and before she could answer, a man's voice spoke in her ear. Rather, it squealed in her ear as if he was trying to overcome a singularly loud and confusing riot of sounds behind him. "Shut up," he yelled. "I tell you, shut up!" It was the veterinarian, Waldo Smith; nobody else had that peculiarly high edge to his voice. The dogs obeyed him—probably, Meade thought, because the high pitch of his voice hurt their sensitive ears.

In any event, he did control them. The growling, snarling, barking tumult behind him ceased. He said in a lower key, "Mrs. Havlock, your dogs are here. They're raising hell with mine. I've got all my dogs in their kennels, so they can't actually fight, but really, Mrs. Havlock—" The snarling, yelping confusion broke out again. He paused, took a deep breath and howled, "SHUT UP!"

"I'm so sorry, Waldo. I don't know how they got out. I'll ask my brother to come for them." But she had a swift and alarming vision of Hoddy in his peculiar purple garment descending on Waldo, and also the garment's effect on her own dogs. A cooing whine came over the telephone. It sounded like Marcelline.

"I've got your little bitch in my arms. Really, Mrs. Havlock..."

Frisky little Marcelline and her frustrated passion for romance. "I'll send my brother right away, Waldo. I am sorry..."

There was some kind of struggle, some squeaky swearing on Waldo's part and the telephone just dropped. Clearly, Marcelline had wriggled out of his arms. She waited, but Waldo didn't pick up the phone again. Yet a man accustomed to forcing down pills past the gleaming white teeth of dogs reluctant to be pilled must have developed some iron in his constitution.

The front door banged open and Hoddy came in, white-faced. "I didn't shoot anybody! I just fired in the air. To scare him off. And somebody ran."

Aunt Chrissy looked at him in horror. "What on earth is that you're wearing?"

"Never mind. Meade, really, I don't think I hit him. I tell you, I just shot in the direction of the gate."

"Why did you shoot at all?" Aunt Chrissy asked. "And what is *that garment*?"

"It's a kaftan. Wonderful," Hoddy said, momentarily diverted. "All wool— I mean, I fired a shot because somebody had been in the house and I wanted him to know that I was awake and armed and all that. He ran."

Meade sighed. "Now you'll have to go to Waldo's and get the dogs. They all streaked down the road to his place, apparently the instant somebody opened the driveway gates."

There was a short silence. Aunt Chrissy then got to the point. "Who opened the gates? And why?"

"To get into the house," Hoddy said shortly. "He must have come through the door of the terrace near the tennis court. It wasn't locked. Unless, of course"—he rubbed his tousled head—"unless nobody came in at all. I mean, unless it was somebody right here in the house. But then, there's only Florrie and John, and I can't see why—"

"*Kindly tell me what you're talking about*" Aunt Chrissy didn't scream, but there was that effect.

"It's nothing, Aunt Chrissy," Meade said hurriedly. "I must have been dreaming. I called Hoddy and told him someone—oh, please go back to bed. Hoddy, you'll have to go and get the dogs."

"I won't," he said.

"You shot at somebody," Aunt Chrissy was always persistent. "So who was it? How do you know you didn't hit him? Or did hit him?"

"If you think there's a corpse out there on the lawn, there isn't." Hoddy was all but shouting. "I tell you, he ran. I won't go for the dogs. Nothing can induce me to go and get those pests."

The telephone rang again. Hoddy, nearest it, picked it up and angrily shouted "Hello!" His voice softened after he had listened. "That's very good of you, Waldo. We'll get them in the morning. Thank you a thousand times."

He hung up and Aunt Chrissy said tartly, "You needn't go overboard thanking him. That's his business, keeping dogs. I don't know what you two have been up to and I want to know."

Hoddy paid no attention to her. "Give me that bottle, Meade. I'll get rid of it." He snatched the bottle out of Meade's hand. He ran out the terrace door, the purple kaftan flapping around his bony ankles, and disappeared.

Aunt Chrissy said flatly, "So. An empty bottle?" and nothing more.

In a moment there was a very faint and faraway tinkle. Hoddy reappeared but was gasping and white. "They'll find my fingerprints on the broken pieces! I forgot to wipe them off. People will say I killed Sam!"

"And did you?" Aunt Chrissy inquired politely.

Seven

Meade took a deep and steadying breath. "You know perfectly well that Hoddy did not kill Sam."

"Somebody did," Aunt Chrissy said.

"What about you?" Hoddy retorted crossly. "You were sitting right beside him. You could have slipped that stuff in his drink."

"But I didn't."

Hoddy, who clearly didn't think she had, sank down on the bottom step of the stairway and put his head in his hands. "If there just wasn't so much money," he said in a kind of moan. "I never thought I'd ever think there was too much money anywhere. And if only Andy hadn't happened to come back just now."

Aunt Chrissy sat down, too, but in a chair, and arranged her pink dressing gown around her as neatly as if she were posing for a portrait. Clearly, she intended to hear everything there was to hear.

"Andy shouldn't have come back to the Cove at all. Not after the shocking way he jilted Meade."

"He didn't jilt me *that way*, Aunt Chrissy. I only thought he'd decided he didn't want me, after all. He simply didn't have any money—"

"He has plenty of money now," Hoddy said. "Or will have. At the very least three hundred million! When Meade marries him. And besides, I know what Andy is doing—and this'll throw you"—he darted an angry glance through his fingers at Aunt Chrissy—"he's in oil."

Aunt Chrissy said acidly, "Sardines? Or a filling station?"

"One day," Hoddy said menacingly, "I'm going to give you the—what you deserve. Even if you are an old lady."

"I'm forty-five," said Aunt Chrissy, who was fifty-eight.

Hoddy said, staring, "All that white hair! And the way you act!"

Aunt Chrissy said airily, "I get attention, don't I? I wouldn't trade white hair for anything! I'm thinking of taking to a cane."

Hoddy stared. "You really are cunning."

"Not at all. Merely diplomatic," Aunt Chrissy said majestically. The door from the terrace opened, bringing in a sweep of cool night air, and Andy who took in at one glance what must have been a rather unusual tableau, said mildly, "Why were you shooting at me, Hoddy?"

"Oh! Was it you who let the dogs out?"

"I didn't even hear the dogs. Just all at once somebody shot at me."

Hoddy said, "I'm glad I missed you."

"So am I," said Andy warmly and then glanced at Meade with a twinkle in his eye but with a certain appreciation, too. "Meade, my darling, aren't you a little chilly?"

"Oh!" cried Aunt Chrissy. She ran to the coat closet and pulled out an overcoat, which she flung around Meade. "*Really!*"

94

The coat was cashmere, one of Sam's, tailored and light, but in some odd way like Sam it seemed to impart no warmth. That's nonsense, Meade told herself, and Hoddy said, "Did you see anybody on the grounds, Andy?"

"No. I just got a shot over my head down by the gate. It startled me," he added dryly.

"And what were you doing there at this time of night?" Aunt Chrissy asked sharply.

Andy's face was curiously thoughtful. "You know, I really don't know why I came. I just felt uneasy; that is, I don't know why, except that"— Andy eyed Aunt Chrissy firmly—"I wanted to be near Meade."

Aunt Chrissy shrugged. "Didn't you intend to come into the house, try to see her, anything?"

"No," Andy said again with that thoughtful look in his eyes. "I don't think I intended anything in particular. I just came. That's all."

"Were the gates open when you came in?" Meade asked. "Yes. And no dogs anywhere."

"You see," Hoddy began to explain, "someone *was* here. Opened the gates, knew the dogs well enough so they simply let him alone and ran off to Waldo's—that's the vet, Andy—"

"Yes, I know. Who came in?"

"We don't know. The door to the little terrace was left unlocked and somebody tried to frame Meade."

"*Frame?* All right, Hoddy, take your aunt upstairs. I want to talk to Meade."

There was a stern command in his voice, as if he were the captain of a ship, Meade thought absurdly. He hadn't spoken like that when he was younger. She watched Hoddy escort Aunt Chrissy upstairs, silently, neither of them looking back, and couldn't believe her eyes. Then she turned to Andy, whose eyes were twinkling again. "That's the kind of job I've had," he said. "Bossy. Come on, let's get out of this drafty hall."

Sam's study was nearest; even when lighted, it

seemed haunted by Sam's presence. Andy did not seem to feel it. He settled her down in an armchair, saw that logs were in the grate and ready for lighting, put a match to the light wood below the logs and began poking around the room for some kind of liquor cabinet. By the time the wood was blazing up toward the logs, he brought a glass of brandy to Meade. "Drink it. We don't want pneumonia on our hands."

"Andy, Andy, you don't know! You don't know—"

"I never will unless you tell me and try to make it short. What is this about framing you?"

She told him everything she could think of, quickly, and then told him of Mrs. Dunham's blackmail threats.

At that, actually a flash of something almost like surprised respect touched his face. "There are all kinds of blackmail, I do believe, but she's got a new wrinkle. Dear me. We'll have to do something about that."

"I won't pay her!"

"Certainly not... Warm enough?"

She nodded; the coat still did not seem to snuggle around her, but the fire was crackling in a comforting way. Andy looked at her for a moment, then reached over, took her bare feet and tucked them under the coat. "There are some things you've got to take into consideration, Meade. The first one is money. Second one is me and the motive we can't deny for wanting you to divorce Sam. So it'll be hard to prove that neither of us had talked to Sam about divorce. There is of course a motive for me to kill my successful rival, the man in possession. But I think the money motive may come first with the law. There's nothing like money as a motive for murder, and Sam had so much money."

"They said I'd probably have three hundred million dollars."

"The whole town knows about that. The settling of such an estate will take time—time and questions and trouble no end. In the meantime, while they're digging away at everything diggable about his business affairs, you and I are going to get married."

"Oh no, Andy. Not so soon after Sam—"

"No, we'll be reasonable about that. You owe it to Sam." He paused and then said in a matter-of-fact way, "But there was no love in your marriage."

"He was kind."

He eyed her thoughtfully. "I believe your stately, firm Aunt Chrissy egged you on to marry him. Come on, now, didn't she?"

"Well, yes . . . I'm not sure. You see, Andy"—a log sent a flare of light swirling upward—"you were so final when you left me . . ."

"I had to make myself like that. I had to convince you, I had to—"

"You convinced me, all right. I was sure you didn't love me. You *could* have asked me to wait for you. You *could* have said that I could go with you wherever you went, share whatever you did. I could struggle along with you if we had to. That's what you ought to have said."

"And you *would* have gone with me?"

"Why, of course!"

"Meade—" He took her hand and pressed it against his lips. Then he said briskly, "I was wrong. I knew it, I think, at the time. That's why I had to make myself sound so determined. After I left you that night, I damn near stopped and went back, but I'd made up my mind to have something to give you first. But then you married. I was a great fool."

"*I* was a fool."

Andy gave her hand a pat. "All right, all right. We've done enough kicking ourselves. What's done's done."

"Truly, Andy, I didn't know what I was doing. I wouldn't let myself stop and think, I had to do something, anything. So—no, that's wrong. I did know what I was doing, in a way. I knew that everyone knew of our engagement. I was hurt and humiliated, and the worst of it was that I kept thinking, 'Here is this big world, it's the only one we know about; Andy is here, in this world with me but I'll never see him again.' Not very bright. But I just swept along with—yes, I suppose, with Aunt Chrissy."

"Who knows a good thing when she sees one," Andy muttered.

"She is alone in the world, Andy. Alone and probably scared. My father dying. All that. Sam was—he came at just the right time. He helped, he really did help. Poor Sam."

Andy frowned at her. "Why poor?"

"I don't think I was ever a good wife to him. I did everything he asked me to do as best I could, but—" Suddenly she sat up. "Andy, there's something about Sam, I mean there was something about him that—I can't describe it—I never understood."

Andy thought for a moment. "I'm not going to take up arms against Sam. There was a time when I could have shot him, but that wore off. Now I don't know how I feel about him except that I know he didn't deserve to die like that. And I'm going to find out who killed him."

"How *can* you? If the police and—"

"Never mind. You've got to go back to bed before those precious pretend-servants of yours come upstairs and really find something to gossip about. How Mrs. Dunham would like to come in just now!"

She sat up. "Andy, Mrs. Dunham could have opened the gates tonight and let the dogs out! They knew her! They like her! She keeps bringing them tidbits from the kitchen. She could have a key to the lower terrace door. I think that is the one she usually uses. She could have come and got into my room and put that bottle—"

Andy's face grew hard. "We'll see about Mrs. Dunham. Now then, I'm going to go upstairs and take the first empty room I find. If you want to stay down here, you can."

"Oh, Andy ..."

The cashmere coat fell away as he held her; she was warm then, warmth flowing through every vein in her body, warm; there was no warmth ever in the world like the warmth of Andy's embrace.

He left the coat on the floor. He put her in her own room and closed the door firmly.

Oddly enough, she slept, and slept deeply so she woke with something like a smile on her lips. When she caught sight of her own face in the bathroom mirror, covered with mist from the shower though it was, she reproved herself. How could she be so happy when her husband had been murdered.

But the day began and ended ominously, so she had no more time to think of such things as possible future happiness.

Florrie brought her breakfast, a tousled Florrie with huge puffs under her eyes. "Reporters," she said and plumped the tray down on a table. "Everywhere. Your brother says not to show your face even at a window. They've got cameras. They keep yelling at Hoddy and he's got the gate bolted. Mr. Garnet is on the phone." She swept the bedside telephone across to Meade and departed, her hair hanging down her shoulders in wisps as if it had never known a brush.

"We'll have to decide immediately, Meade," Brice said.

"Decide?"

"That is, I've already made some arrangements to save you any worry, and I do hope they suit you." He paused as if reading from notes. "Tomorrow at two: St. Stephen's Church. Father Selmore, a simple sermon, short and simple. That's what

99

Sam would have liked. There's a little trouble here, though, Meade. The governor insists upon giving a eulogy. It's a political move on his part. Outrageous really. Sam was doing his best to get me elected. The governor's fighting for his job. I suppose he wants people to say what a great man he is, giving a eulogy to his political foe. He's a terrific talker. Goes on and on."

"Tell him I said...I don't know what."

"I do," Brice said. "I already have. I told him that Sam had left the most explicit instructions in the event of his death. Merely a few psalms read, and a prayer. A prayer at the graveside. Grave in the cemetery of St. Stephen's, alongside his father's—and all the Havlocks'. Space there for you, too," Brice said practically but not very tactfully. "Now then, I've put all this in the papers, and I said the family would prefer no flowers and no donations. Does that suit you?"

"Oh yes. That is, Sam might have wished some donations—"

"Not from other people. He'd have given donations himself, but he would never put other people in the position of having to give. Often he would start a fund with a good big wallop of a check, but he'd never ask it of others. Well, how about the coffin, closed or open?"

"Oh..." She took a deep, sorrowful breath. "Closed, Brice. Closed! He'd have wanted that."

"Thought so too. That is what I told them. Agnes said I should let you choose the coffin, but I felt you'd rather have her choose it or me or—"

"Oh yes. Yes. Besides—Brice, the reporters—we seem to be practically besieged."

"Naturally. What can you expect? A man like Sam! Well, keep the gates closed. Can't Hoddy do something about keeping them out?"

"He's trying. Wait a minute!"

Andy had flung the door open. "Who are you talking to?"

"Brice Garnet."

"Ask him to get some police out here. A photographer climbed up the slope just now and fell on the terrace stairs. I'm afraid he only broke his camera. They're like bees swarming. Tell him to hurry." He vanished and she heard him running back downstairs.

"Was that Andy Brooke? What's he doing there? Good God, Meade! Don't you realize that Sam was murdered? People, gossips, are already saying that after Andy returns, Sam is murdered right away. You come into money. The police will put everything together."

"You won't let them, Brice!"

He said wearily, "I'll try. After all, there's really no evidence."

Mrs. Dunham. The small empty vial. The fact that someone had entered her room. She paused, thought and told him about the bottle. She didn't tell him of Mrs. Dunham's threat. There was too dangerous a truth in that to tell anybody.

"Why didn't you call the police?"

"The police—I suppose it just never occurred to us. We thought we heard someone run outside. Hoddy searched the grounds, Andy came, he was somewhere near the gates. Hoddy shot—"

"At Andy?"

"No, no. Hoddy didn't know he was here."

"All right. Call the police now. Tell them the reporters are all around the place. Tell them about the empty bottle last night, Hoddy's shooting. But *don't* tell them Andy was hanging around. I think you'd better tell them the dogs were let out. Someone the dogs know must have opened the big gates. Although that's not much evidence. If a stranger came along with a good big steak and tossed it on the road just outside the gates and then opened the gates— Have they been trained not to accept food from a stranger?"

"No," she said in a small voice.

101

"Go call the police now. Agnes has gone to New York to get mourning clothes for you. Good-bye."

Mourning clothes. Another thing she had never thought about.

She had scarcely swallowed a cup of coffee when he rang again; she answered.

"Meade?"

"Yes, Brice."

"Are there any extensions on your phone? Of course there must be. Do you think anybody is listening in?"

"I don't know. I usually hear a sort of click when that happens accidentally."

"This might not be accidental. I meant to ask you before. Do you object if I have that couple Sam employed—well, if I find out something about their backgrounds? I mean—"

"You mean put detectives on their trail!"

"Why not? They're a very peculiar couple. Why would they accept household labor when both say they are actors?"

"Because they needed the money."

"Maybe. But with your permission, Meade, I'd like to make sure of—oh, something more definite about their backgrounds. Frankly, I don't like them."

Neither do I, thought Meade. And certainly John—both of them seemed terrified. "Oh, all right," she said wearily, and then a spark of misplaced mischief entered her. "What do you think of Mrs. Dunham, Brice?"

His voice changed. "Oh, Mrs. Dunham...she's all right. She's of the old school. The few times she's worked for us, the food has been excellent. You can count on her. Good-bye."

Count on her for some fine and fancy blackmailing, Meade thought irritably. Yet she didn't want to tell Brice about the attempted blackmail and thus the exact facts of her meeting with Andy at the tennis court. Somehow, some way, Andy would stop Mrs. Dunham.

Besides, as had occurred to her before, whatever Mrs. Dunham could tell the police, Haggerty had already some notion about and he was right. Only the exact words she and Andy had used were at all likely to come as news to him. (But that was definite talk of divorce!) Yet Haggerty hadn't seemed to turn any particular attention to Andy.

The day turned sulky, with the Sound a sullen, quiet gray. Several blue uniforms appeared from the foggy wreaths of mist; cameras and marauding reporters disappeared. Sometime during the day Hoddy took the station wagon and returned with the dogs, who showed no signs of regret. Andy had apparently left early that morning and did not return; the afternoon crept on toward evening.

Aunt Chrissy, after considerable delving in wardrobes and skirmishing with Florrie about iron and ironing boards, turned up in dead black.

Meade had taken refuge in the formal living room and closed the door. It seemed, that foggy day, rather like the salon of a ship, high above everything, floating through misty gray clouds. She was curled up on a sofa, wishing Andy would come, wishing she had not so much to think of, wishing the next day were over with, wishing all the questions were answered, wishing, wishing, when Aunt Chrissy sailed in, white hair freshly done, black dress a very smart sheath which showed much of her really good figure, a fact of which she was fully conscious. She gave herself an approving look in the big gilt-framed mirror over the marble fireplace. "Black always was becoming to me," she said. "I haven't worn this since your father's death. I can't imagine why."

She did look almost regal. She turned around and surveyed Meade. "For heaven's sake, child!

103

Slacks and sneakers and a sweater. Have you no sense of decorum?"

"You have enough for two," Meade said more impertinently than she would ever have spoken in her childhood.

Aunt Chrissy paid no attention. "It's too late now. Haggerty is here, and Brice. I heard them talking. Something about a bottle and that vet, Waldo. Haggerty says he ought to arrest you and Brice says no, he mustn't."

Meade had jumped to her feet. Odd, for she really felt like stone, as if she couldn't move.

"Then they saw me on the stairs, so I came to find you. They're in Sam's study."

"Mrs. Havlock," said Chief Haggerty from the doorway.

Eight

Meade couldn't sink down into the pillows. She did wish she hadn't been wearing a sweater and slacks; it didn't seem right to be arrested in a sweater and slacks. And she was just as silly as Aunt Chrissy. She said stiffly, "Yes, Chief Haggerty."

He said quite unexpectedly, "Don't be scared."

She swallowed. "What—"

"I'm not going to arrest you. Not now."

"Arrest," Meade whispered.

Chief Haggerty looked very sober. "I think I can take my time. People in this town know me. Trust my judgment."

Aunt Chrissy, who up to then had stood in stunned but elegant dignity, suddenly said, "What utter nonsense! Arrest!"

But Chief Haggerty couldn't, surely he couldn't

in his heart believe that Meade, a girl he had seen through her childhood, had suddenly turned into a particularly cruel murderess. Yet facts are facts and nobody knows that any better than the chief of police of any small town. Brice had followed him and came to Meade, taking her hand. "Chief Haggerty, I think Mrs. Havlock ought to know what all this is about."

Chief Haggerty replied precisely, "The vet, young Waldo Smith, had some of this stuff that killed Sam. It was in what he calls his surgery. He'd been operating on one of Mrs. Havlock's dogs. She waited in the drugstore, he said, while he removed a cyst from the dog and sewed up the wound. Then she came back when he told her to, about an hour later, and got the dog. Waldo was in another room, washing his hands or something. Anyway, he didn't happen to check over his drug cabinet until yesterday. Now, Waldo,"—the chief shook his head—"is not what you'd call tidy about his supplies. I know he is a very good vet and we are lucky to have him. He's really got his heart in his job. But he's got no sense of order in those back rooms, bottles, cases, empty pasteboard boxes, empty bottles, the place needs a good turning out. Those front rooms, the waiting room and the operating room and what he calls the recovery room, those rooms are all spick-and-span. But beyond that—I don't see how he ever finds anything. There are wall cabinets he says he almost never locks, why should he? That's what he said, 'Why lock them when it's only dog medicine and no dog is likely to come and help himself?'"

Haggerty got out a handkerchief and mopped his face as if his interview with Waldo had been a little exhausting, as Meade could well imagine it had been. "But he's sure he left the bottle of this number something-or-other stuff out on a table while he was working with Meade's dog. Now he can't find the bottle. He didn't dare use much on the dog, barely enough to put her to sleep for a little

106

while. He was careful enough about that. Showed me his notes, neat as a pin, the amount of the dosage and the time it took to work and the time it took for the dog to get her senses again, all that. He was almost in tears by that time. But the point is, the bottle he had used for your dog, Meade, had disappeared. He hadn't used much for the dog, so there may have been more than enough left to kill a man. He didn't notice when you came back for your dog, Meade. He handed her over to you and dashed off on some emergency call."

He took a deep breath and then said heavily, "The smashed bottle has been found on the lower slope below the terrace, near where we found the cherries and the remains of a cocktail glass. We've pieced it together. We can't really make out fingerprints, but Waldo Smith says it's the same sort of bottle."

Oh, Hoddy, why didn't you hide it some place else, any place, Meade thought desperately.

Hagerty said, "I guess that's all I can say. Only—if you don't mind, I want to leave a squad car with two of my men around tonight. I'm a little short-handed, but it's for your own safety. You see"—he was rather apologetic—"somehow word has got out among the townspeople—you know how news travels—and since Sam was so popular with everyone, there's been a little mean talk. Just among the hotheads, you know. Wouldn't amount to anything, but maybe a bit of rock throwing, shouts, attempts to get into the grounds, that kind of thing. I don't intend to let it happen."

With that he disappeared.

Brice said dryly that Andy would do Meade no favor by hanging around like this, when Andy came into the room.

"I know, Brice," said Andy, "and I agree. But just for a moment—"

"No stopping you, huh?" Brice shook his head but went out after the chief.

Meade sat back in the green velvet cushions of

107

the sofa. The whole thing seemed like a nightmare. Even Andy's face, as he approached her, was part of a nightmare. "Andy, they can't arrest me."

Andy spoke cheerfully but looked sober. "The point is, you are now free until—you will be free, darling, because you didn't do it."

Aunt Chrissy swept up in her black elegance. "You two fools," she hissed piercingly. "Do you have to sit there together and look like that at a time like this!"

Brice came back into the room as she spoke. "She's quite right. I forgot to tell you, Meade, Agnes will bring you some black dresses tomorrow morning. Cars and everything else have been arranged. It's got to be rather ceremonious. Sam was so well known. You'll simply have to put up with the whole thing. Good-night, Meade. Remember, we are at the other end of the phone." He went away.

"He's right about that," Andy said gravely. "The whole town is talking, you know. My cousin Isabel has a third ear, tuned for gossip. Believe me, if you lock your door at night, close the curtains and sneeze, she's likely to ask you next morning how your cold is." He laughed shortly. "But she's a good old girl, just the same. She's all for you. So am I," he said and took Meade tightly in his arms.

"Oh, Andy, how could I have been so silly! Everything happened so quickly. It was all mixed up in my mind—if I have any," she added gloomily.

Hoddy opened the door. "Don't you ever stop smooching?" he asked in disgust. "Honestly, at such a time! Meade and talk of arrest, and while I think Haggerty knows in his heart that she couldn't have murdered Sam, still...if anybody else saw you..."

Mrs. Dunham had seen them once and had heard them; and now Mrs. Dunham would have to prepare what she would certainly call a collation, after the services tomorrow. Funeral baked meats—the gloomy phrase floated in Meade's memory even as a tumult of barks, howls and frustrated yelps roared out in the distance.

"I locked them up," Hoddy said. "They didn't like it. One of them bit me!" He rolled up one leg of his sloppy jeans and showed a small circle of red imprints. Meade looked at it quickly, but none of the dents had broken the skin. "I think you'll live," she said to Hoddy. "But thanks for bringing them home."

"There'll be a squad car around tonight. Haggerty told me. So that's good. But honestly, Andy, I don't think you ought to hang around here so much."

"Oh yes, you're right," Andy said soberly. "Everybody's right."

"Wait a minute, Andy. You did say that you're in the oil business, didn't you?" Hoddy asked.

Andy nodded, the beginning quirk of a smile on his lips as if he knew what was coming.

"Isn't it something to do with oil wells? When we met in Paris you said you'd been out in the Middle East doing something or other—"

"Cut it short, Hoddy. Yes, I'm an engineer, specialty oil wells. Managed to do a decent job for some potentates. Saved a little capital. Now I'm on my own with a batch of oil leases. Some of them—wells, I mean—may come in and some may not. It's always a risk."

He looked at Meade and repeated, "A big risk! You can keep on putting every last cent you have in your leases and not get a smell of oil. But then, I've tried to use the expertise I've gathered. I think I can manage to make a living. But not three hundred million dollars!"

His voice was light; his eyes very sober. Meade replied to the sobriety. "I don't need that much money."

"You don't think you do, but you're accustomed to it."

Meade said slowly, after a moment, "You don't

want a wife who has so much money, Andy."

He reverted to one of his light moods. "A wife with money strikes me as a very good thing, especially if you're a poet or a painter or..." His face hardened. "But I intend to support my own wife. So you can throw that money out the window if you want to."

"No, no, she can't do that!" Hoddy intervened, almost hysterically. "Andy, you don't know what you're talking about!"

"Usually I do," said Andy, a spark of anger in his eyes.

"Well, but think of the things that money can do."

Andy was still deeply angry. "For you?"

"Well... some of it would help."

The anger left Andy's face. "How?"

"Oh—anything. But you could give me a job, couldn't you?"

"What can you do?" Andy asked politely.

"I'll do anything you tell me to do," Hoddy burst out. "Dig for the oil if you want me to."

"Digging for oil is not child's play."

"Oh, I know, I know, but I'll try."

"Hoddy, we don't know what's going to happen," Meade said seriously. "Don't you realize that I may have to go on trial for Sam's murder?"

"Of course I realize it, but you'll never go on trial. Now listen. It stands to reason that this is an unusual case. They'll keep right on hunting down every scrap of evidence that they can find. Sam was so well known that they really don't want to bring his wife into court on a murder charge. Yet the evidence against you so far is too strong to overlook..."

"Hoddy," Meade said desperately, "will you stop talking? You don't know a thing about what the police will do."

"I do, too, know something. I've read the newspapers. When somebody's murdered they don't wait to get the whole case in order; they just arrest the suspect, if the evidence is strong enough, and pop him into jail. They didn't do that with you because of your and Sam's standing." Hoddy fell into one of his infrequent spasms of sound reflection. "Besides, Haggerty doesn't believe you killed him. Makes a difference. There's somebody at the front door," he said and quick as an eel vanished.

Andy laughed outright. "You needn't worry about that young man, Meade. He'll get somewhere. I can't say I know where exactly, but somewhere." He rubbed his forehead wearily. "Somehow we must resolve all this— What's that racket in the hall?"

He opened the door. There was a commotion in the hall, heavy footsteps, Aunt Chrissy was giving directions, everyone seemed to be giving directions, and the dogs were raising particular, frustrated hell from the kennels. Meade went to the door; she was greeted by voices, thuds and smells, hothouse smells. There were vases of flowers, arrangements of flowers, tubs of flowers. In spite of the family request for no flowers or donations, the hall looked like a florist's shop.

"The men got so many orders they thought they might as well deliver a whole truckload at once," Hoddy said, eying the masses of flowers rather possessively and proudly as if he had brought them all himself. "Make quite a show, don't they?" He disentangled a white envelope from a small but important-looking tree of gardenias, which sweetened the air with their heavy fragrance. "H'mmm, 'Officers and Directors of the—something or other...'" He went on, choosing cards, "Every darn one of them from some bank or some business outfit. Funny, nothing from anybody in the Cove."

"They'll go to the church," Andy assured Meade so soberly and quickly that she knew he meant to tell her that she had friends in the Cove and that

111

they would stick with her, no matter what happened.

The doorbell rang. There were in fact two doorbells, one small electric bell which gave forth a shrill tinkle, one a big iron contraption which, when pulled up and let drop, practically roused the whole town with its harsh and, it seemed to Meade, very doleful tones.

"Sounds like an army," Andy said.

Hoddy put his hands over his ears and ran to open the door. The clanging stopped and Hoddy ushered in not an army, but Waldo Smith. Aunt Chrissy hovered in the background for an instant and then disappeared as if nothing this individual had to say could possibly interest her. Indeed, Waldo looked extraordinarily shabby. Sometimes Meade wondered how he could be clothed in perfectly whole and solid materials, suitable to a country gentleman in fact, and still manage to look as if he had just crept out from some very dirty freight car. The dogs' distant yells sounded like a cageful of tigers, deprived of their daily meal, and yet were actually expressions of affection for Waldo.

Waldo stopped and bowed, went back to the door, opened it and whistled.

It was such a piercing whistle that Meade put her own hands over her ears. Andy said, "For God's sake, Waldo!" But then he laughed quietly as the dogs shut up all at once. It was like magic.

Waldo turned around and closed the door. "It's always been like that," he said almost apologetically. "I don't know why. Ever since I was a kid—"

"That whistle ought to stop a train," said Hoddy unpleasantly. "My ears are ringing."

Waldo looked troubled but interested. "Are they really, Hoddy? You see, I've been experimenting in—but it would bore you—the acoustical properties of—"

"Waldo," said Andy, "did you want to see Mrs. Havlock?"

"Oh yes. Yes. I've been so worried. Ever since Chief Haggerty came to my office and asked all those questions and I had to answer of course...Mrs. Havlock," he said miserably, "I wouldn't do anything to cast suspicion on you!"

"I know that. Sit down, Waldo," Meade said gently.

He sank down on the very edge of a gilded French armchair; his hands were scrubbed so constantly that they were red; they were clasped between his thin knees. "You see, somebody sent me a consignment of that stuff. It's still in such an experimental stage that none of the big doctors around here are about to use it. Some of the medical schools have tried it, very cautiously—oh, you don't want to hear all this. The point is, I got some, The Hiddle School of Medicine permitted me to have a small supply with the understanding that I was to keep very exact records, use it under completely controlled conditions and then report to them. You've no idea," he said, straightening his thin little body with some degree of dignity, "how some of the medical schools and even some of the important doctors really take an interest in information we lowly vets can give them."

"I wouldn't call you lowly," Andy said. "Now, when Haggerty asked you if you had used it for Marcelline..."

Waldo sagged again. "Well, of course I said yes. So he said, 'Show me the bottle,' and I couldn't because it wasn't there. I explained that I had used just a little on Marcelline—and you saw yourself, Mrs. Havlock, with what good results—"

"Go on," said Andy.

Waldo shot him a frightened look. "I had to tell the truth. I had used it and then I took Marcelline back to what I call my recovery room. Well, then the chief of police asked me point-blank if Mrs. Havlock had been in the room. I had to say yes. He asked me so many questions I got all confused, but the main thing was that—well, you were in the operating room alone for a minute or two, Mrs. Havlock. You waited there with Marcelline while I went to open the recovery room and wash my hands. Then you said you would go over to the drugstore and get a sandwich. I knew that if that stuff worked all right, Marcelline could be taken home in an hour or so. And it did. And you did—I mean, bring her home. But I don't remember anything more about that bottle. Somebody called in and said there was a mad dog roaming around her place and I had to go and fetch him—really the dogcatcher's job, but the dog wasn't mad at all, just very thirsty and naturally cross and—"

Andy stemmed the flow. "Are your storerooms locked now?"

Waldo flinched. "Yes! Since this morning. All my supplies."

"After you talked to Chief Haggerty?"

"Yes. But I knew Mrs. Havlock—"

"You might have kept your mouth shut about it," Andy said, but in a resigned way. "I suppose you couldn't."

"Oh, I couldn't. Really I couldn't. Not with Chief Haggerty questioning me like that, going through my whole place. I really ... but I didn't mean—oh, I don't know what to do."

Andy said slowly, "It's done, Waldo. And Mrs. Havlock didn't take that bottle. But somebody did take it. Do you have any idea who that could be?"

Waldo's thin eyebrows went up almost to his slick, thin hair. "Why, I—I don't know. But I'll think. Yes. I'll look at my books, too. I'll think back. I'll work on it. I really will work on it."

He made a move to leave, but Andy stopped him. "Wait a minute, Waldo. What in your opinion are

114

the general effects of this whatever-you-call-it drug?"

"Oh, that's simple. It's a relaxer. Relaxes muscles so it makes it much easier for the vet, or the surgeon, to work. The only trouble is, so far—at least as far as I know—there hasn't been time or opportunity to get complete data. I mean, it's possible to give too much or too little."

"The lab boys say it would relax the heart if you gave too much."

"Oh dear me, yes. Works almost as fast as cyanide. Heart, lungs, all the muscles. Even the brain. Oh dear, yes."

So a man would simply slide off a balustrade, down a slope of rocks and shrubs, into water and have not the consciousness, the will or strength to help himself.

"It's the only explanation, Meade," Andy said. "And there's one comfort—slight, but a comfort. Clearly, Sam had such a dose of this stuff that it went right to work. Sam didn't know anything that happened. Remember, he didn't even speak."

"No," Waldo said. "No, he wouldn't have been able to make a sound. That's another thing the surgeons are beginning to like about this stuff. The patient doesn't toss around and murmur and it makes their job much easier—safer too. It has a rather distinctive, bitter taste. I tried a drop on my tongue. I gave it to Marcelline in a chunk of cheese. But if I'd thought twice—"

"You didn't," Andy said rather sharply, but then as Waldo's face became tragically woebegone he said, "Thank you, Waldo. You were right to come and tell us."

Andy took him out. Hoddy said gloomily, "Best witness the prosecution could have. I mean, if it comes to a trial. You were there, Meade. He was out of the room. The bottle turned up in your room. And was found smashed but identifiable on the slope

115

down to the Sound. I shouldn't have thrown it there. Such a damn fool thing to do!"

"It's done," Meade said wearily.

Andy came back in the room, accompanied by Aunt Chrissy and a terrific wave of perfume. Lilies and gardenias seemed the main fragrances, although there were gentler whiffs of lilacs. Meade could see through the open door another two or three men in workman's jeans carrying and placing pots of flowers. "Another load has arrived," Andy said rather grimly. "They want to know what to do with them."

"Tell 'em—" muttered Hoddy but Aunt Chrissy caught it as swiftly as she had when he was fourteen.

"That will do, Hoddy!" She turned to Meade. "I suggest the terrace. There's simply nowhere else. The place is full."

She swept out again and luckily closed the door behind her, for Andy took Meade tightly in his arms. "The squad car will be around the place tonight. I'll go back to Cousin Isabel's. There is a phone right at my bedside. Darling—"

"I don't see how you can stand all this smooching," said Hoddy austerely and stalked out, leaving the door open so they could see him stop, scrutinize the various tubs and vases, and carefully choose a white carnation which he forced into a snagged space in his dirty brown shirt, then walk away as jauntily as any Edwardian dandy.

But after Andy had gone, after they had managed a kind of pick-up supper from the table in the rarely used breakfast room, Meade hurried to her room and locked the door, not against a figure sliding through the darkness that night, not really, she told herself, just because she felt better with it locked. She sat down at her desk, she went to her dressing table, she wandered to the chaise longue. She wound up flat on the bed, hands behind her head, staring at the ceiling. They said

116

that innocent people were never convicted. Or at least seldom convicted.

Sleep eventually did catch up with her, for when she awoke rain was streaking the windows, through which morning light shone in. Florrie was knocking at the door. Meade struggled upward and unlocked the door. Florrie brought coffee and a very hard roll and looked surprisingly neat; her coarse hair had been combed up and pinned. Her eyes were lowered so she did not look at Meade, who discovered herself still in sweater and slacks. She thought, Good heavens, I've slept in my clothes, whatever is the matter with Florrie—all in one second.

The tray plunked down on the bedside table. Meade brought herself to a partial sense of time and place. "What's happened, Florrie? You look different."

At once Florrie's eyes flashed up almost defiantly. "Why shouldn't I? John is gone."

Nine

"Gone," Meade repeated. "Gone where?"

"How should I know?"

There was something in her voice, her whole attitude, that was curiously smug, almost self-satisfied. Yet when Meade stared at her, trying to understand her reaction, Florrie began to weep in great sobs, hands over her eyes, breast heaving. "You killed him, too!" she cried. "Oh, I know you did! You thought he saw you put that stuff in Sam's, I mean Mr. Havlock's, drink. So you got rid of John!"

"Florrie, stop that screaming! Take your hands from your eyes."

Florrie uttered a resounding sob—a stage sob, Meade thought unkindly—and took her hands from her eyes, which were truly red and watery. Fingers in them? Meade thought again skeptically. All the same, if John had gone, then why? And where? And what could they do about it? Report it to the police of course. She reached for the telephone.

"Oh, I let the police know at once! There's more trouble, too. Mrs. Dunham has disappeared."

"Now listen, Florrie, you must be making up all this—"

"Don't I know when John disappears? He's gone and nobody knows where. And Mrs. Dunham's gone too."

"I don't think they eloped," Meade said before she could stop herself. No sense in turning into a shrew, especially at such a moment.

But Florrie merely shrugged with a return of her usual saucy manner. "John likes her cooking but not Mrs. Dunham herself." On her way out, she paused in the doorway and said, "I don't see how anybody could like Mrs. Dunham."

I'm with you there, Meade thought, and then Hoddy hurtled into the room. "Good God, Meade, John has disappeared and so has Mrs. Dunham. You don't suppose they eloped?"

Meade repressed a very untimely giggle. "Neither Forrie nor I think that."

Hoddy came up with another notion. "Do you think somebody thought John knew too much and killed him? And Mrs. Dunham, too?"

Mrs. Dunham—and the funeral supper! There was too much to think about or speculate about, and there were all those people arriving for the funeral who would have to be fed afterward. "Give me the phone." Hoddy handed her the phone and leather-bound address book. She found the number for the caterer who occasionally had managed affairs when Sam wished to give a very large party. She got the manager, after giving her name. He was all solicitude, he was all sympathy, he regretted the loss of her husband and he would be

120

on hand at the Cove himself, with food and waiters.

Hoddy looked at her with unflattering surprise. "I didn't know you were so efficient," he said, and added, "So everything about supper is all right. But this business of John and Mrs. Dunham. You don't suppose they *have* eloped, do you?"

"No!"

"I heard Florrie on the phone this morning telling Haggerty about John. Haggerty came around and talked to her, didn't talk to me or Aunt Chrissy. Then somebody who lives near that cottage Mrs. Dunham rented down by the water phoned while Haggerty was here and asked to speak to him, and from what I heard, she told him Mrs. Dunham's car was standing out in front of her house, where she never leaves it overnight, and the house door was wide open and lights on but no Mrs. Dunham anywhere."

Meade looked at her bed and decided the only thing she wanted to do at that moment was crawl back in bed and pull the pillows over her head. Hoddy said, "You'd better get busy. There are all kinds of telegrams and messages, and somebody's got to give us some kind of lunch before Sam's funeral. Funerals are bad enough at any time but on an empty stomach—"

"Go fix lunch yourself," Meade snapped. "You can put together a sandwich as well as anybody. I want to talk to Brice and Agnes."

It was a great relief to hear Agnes' tranquil self-possessed voice over the phone. "I was just going to call you. I'm sending some black dresses—"

"Agnes, listen—" She told her bluntly the only things she knew. John had disappeared. Mrs. Dunham was not to be found and she had left her car, which she loved, and her house, lights on, nothing locked up, just left it.

Agnes was a practical housekeeper. "First things first. You'll have to get a caterer from the city—"

"I know. I have. They'll be here and see to everything."

"Good girl!" Agnes, too, sounded surprised. Didn't anybody expect Meade to behave like a person on her own account, not just a pretty young thing who wore the clothes and jewels Sam gave her and went to great public dinners with him and did everything he asked her to do, even if it meant making a speech or two herself?

Thinking it over, however, she could see that even a close friend like Agnes might have had just that opinion. She hadn't known Agnes until after her marriage to Sam; since he and Brice were such old friends, naturally Agnes had taken an interest in Sam's young bride, and the interest had grown into real affection. She could count on Agnes. Indeed, it occurred to her that possibly Agnes had been so strong in her defense of Meade that she had all but forced Brice to undertake to defend Meade himself—if a trial for murder did eventually take place. A trial for murder! She couldn't let herself think of that and couldn't stop it.

The morning passed swiftly; Meade tried on the three dresses that were brought almost at once by Agnes' part-time gardener; every one of them was the right size and fit as perfectly as a dress bought off the rack could fit. Luckily the most decorous of the dresses, with long sleeves and a high neck, fit the best. In fact, Meade thought vaguely, glancing at her own reflection in the long mirror, it fit almost too well. She did have a good figure, but she wasn't sure it should be shown off so advantageously at Sam's funeral. There were three hats, too, and a long black veil. She pinned up her hair, tried on all the hats and chose a snug one that was not likely to slip during what Hoddy called the ups-and-downs of a religious service.

Hoddy had done his best with sandwiches, he told her, and Aunt Chrissy said they'd better eat if it choked them. The flowers had all gone, but their scent lingered, and Aunt Chrissy had neatly snipped off all the cards and put a rubber band around them. "Every single one will have to be answered by hand," she said firmly. "Now get your hat and veil on, Meade. I hear the cars coming."

Hoddy led Meade ceremoniously to the car; the undertakers looked preternaturally solemn. A long black hearse was waiting at the big gates; it was covered with flowers, and another car following it was also heaped with flowers.

The cortege began its slow and solemn way to the church and Hoddy said peevishly, "I don't see why on earth John would take it into his head to disappear just now. Or Mrs. Dunham either."

Suddenly Meade thought, Sometimes black-mailers do have unexpected and terrible ends.

Eventually all the solemn ceremonies were concluded; the last few distinguished guests were leaving, having eaten rather largely of pâté, watercress sandwiches and assorted hot patties. Following soft whispers from the waiters ("Tea or coffee, sir? Or a cool drink?"), glasses, decanters and ice had appeared on the table on the terrace and been put to full use.

Her lips were very tired of saying "Thank you ...thank you..." She had surreptitiously flexed her right hand and shaken hands again—and again and again. She had not seen Mr. Bacon at the services, but he came forward amid the confusion of people at the house; he was accompanied by another man, one of his firm, he said in dry introduction. The other man looked at her with a mixture of curiosity and surmise which, remembering it later, gave her a feeling of being on trial then and there. Mr. Bacon barely took her hand,

123

murmured something and both men left. It struck her later that there was an air of chill reserve about the lawyer as if he too were trying to judge her—faithful wife or murderess. Dreadful words! But then, Mr. Bacon, and through him other members of the firm, would have been apprised of the entire situation as Chief Haggerty—and most of the Cove—knew it.

All at once it was over, and out of a kind of weary mist Andy's Cousin Isabel came forward. She took both Meade's hands. "Come out on the terrace, child. Fresh air—rest—come along."

Meade went with her. In a way Cousin Isabel was as autocratic as Aunt Chrissy; the two of them did not agree about most of the civic affairs in which they interested themselves; yet like two rival rulers who must agree or lose a kingdom, they forced themselves to act as a team on any program suggested. Isabel wasn't really Andy's cousin, it was just simpler to call her that. She put Meade down in a long wicker chair. "Now put your feet up."

Cousin Isabel was aware of most of the things that went on in the village, so was Aunt Chrissy. But to give them credit where it was due, while they might gossip with each other, as a rule they kept their special gems of drama to themselves. Now Cousin Isabel said, surprisingly, "You must have a good slug of liquor. Oh, here's Hoddy."

Hoddy bounced along with a glass in his hand. "Bourbon," he said. "I made it strong. You need it."

"Why, that's right, Hoddy," said Cousin Isabel with probably the first approving look she had given Hoddy since he started clumping over her lawn in football shoes, as he often did because it was the short way home from school.

Isabel settled down on a wicker footstool near Meade. "Now then, dear, you carried everything

124

off very nicely. I'll tell Andy how well you did."

Andy had not been at the funeral. At Meade's questioning look Isabel said, "He felt he couldn't come. That's all he would say. My private opinion is—well, as a matter of fact, he thinks Mrs. Dunham was murdered. Now don't look like that. Swallow your drink before anyone notices."

She gulped down the bourbon, which was not very strongly diluted with water. Her throat stung. Isabel went on in a low voice, "He said not to tell you that, so," she added as if it were a natural conclusion, "so I did."

After a moment Meade asked, "Why?"

"I thought you ought to know."

"But why does he think she was murdered?"

Cousin Isabel looked out over the tranquil blue and gold of the Sound and said only, "He told me to tell you that he would be away for a few days. He didn't know how long. But I must be sure to tell you that much."

So, Meade thought, coming to her senses all at once, as if she'd been in a particularly unbelievable dream all that day, Andy was going to try to do some investigating on his own. He was going to try to find out— What *could* he find out? All the facts that anybody could discover were already known, particularly by the police.

"What are the police doing about Mrs. Dunham?" she said, staring down at the glass in her hand but aware of the rustle of Isabel's neat gray silk as she rose when she saw Aunt Chrissy coming out to join them. "I don't know, dear. Yes, Chrissy, I've been trying to get this child to go upstairs and rest. She's done so well."

"It was horrible," said Aunt Chrissy. "Horrible! Everybody in that church and all along the sidewalks and right here in our own house knows that Meade is all but accused of murdering Sam." Her voice shook. Aunt Chrissy was not as a rule

125

sympathetic or emotional. "All of them were watching her and watching all of us and it was horrible!"

Isabel said, "It was worse for Meade. But she's going to be freed completely. I'm perfectly sure of that!" She gave Meade a swift kiss and went away, leaving a gentle wave of Chanel No. 5 behind her.

Aunt Chrissy said grudgingly, "I've always said Isabel could be a help. Agnes, too."

Agnes came out on the terrace, her lovely, tranquil·eyes resting on Meade, "Come upstairs now, Meade."

Once upstairs, Agnes made her take off her sleek black dress and put on a dressing gown and lie down. She had carried the glass of bourbon and water with her, which she put in Meade's hand. She shook out the black dress and looked at it doubtfully. "I was in a hurry. I had to take what I could find. The vendeuse and her two models were so kind. They had read the papers. They felt very sorry for you. They all sent their sympathy. I was afraid this dress was just a little too—oh, revealing, so to speak, but still it had a high neck and long sleeves and I shudder to think what the Cove would have said if you turned up at Sam's funeral in short sleeves." She hung the dress in the closet. "You're not to worry about Mrs. Dunham. Brice says she must have taken it into her head to look for some other job snd she'll turn up."

"But they say she left her car standing out in front of her house. Doors of the house open, lights on..."

"The police will find her. Don't worry about her. Brice says he's moving heaven and earth to get the inquiry over with, get you cleared."

"What about his campaign? This will delay him."

Agnes sat down and looked quietly at the carpet. "He doesn't think so. And he owes it to Sam. Didn't you know Sam had given Brice a big campaign fund? Well, he did. Brice will get you free and cleared, I promise you that. So now—good night, my dear."

To Meade's vague surprise it was already twilight. Aunt Chrissy brought her supper on a tray; it consisted of leftovers from the afternoon's obligatory reception. "There's plenty. The caterer of course knows that Sam—I mean you—would pay anything he asked. Sam was one of his best customers. Now eat."

Left alone, Meade looked at the sandwiches, the tiny patties of hot chicken and mushrooms, even the half bottle of white wine somebody, probably Hoddy, had put on the tray. She couldn't eat; she couldn't possibly eat.

She took one bite and then another and then ate as if she'd been starved for months. She drank every drop of the wine. Gradually she began to feel not quite normal, but more like Meade Havlock. Who had been Meade Forrest—and would have been Meade Brooke if both she and Andy hadn't been rash, so stupid and young.

There was no use speculating on what Andy could be doing, what evidence he was trying to unearth. She went to sleep.

Sometime during the night she was dimly aware of Hoddy's tiptoeing in, pulling an eiderdown up over her and taking away the tray; she mumbled something and went back to sleep as if drugged.

The next day and the next passed and nothing, it seemed, happened. In fact, a number of things happened, but Meade did not know that.

Brice and Hoddy helped her with the ever demanding task of sorting what papers Sam had kept in his big desk. There were not many, really; he kept all business records in his New York office and Miss Bellamy was acquainted with those. There were merely a few notes of speeches which he had delivered or was about to deliver, all typed out by the efficient Miss Bellamy before she had left on vacation; stacks of notepaper and envelopes, engraved simply *Havlock* as if that were quite enough, for there was not even a return address; various oddments of stamps, note pads, pencils, pens; no engagement book—which Brice frowned over; "I don't see how Sam remembered everything. But he always did." Certainly there was no diary which might have given some clue to his murder, although that was a faint hope, expressed by Hoddy without conviction.

It took time. After a while Meade decided she would let Hoddy see to Sam's clothes; some of them could go to Thrift Shops and charity; she wouldn't think about that yet.

She began to write letters of thanks, formal notes for the most part to names which were strange to her; a few she recognized. Her hand was tired and she was tired, and once she and Hoddy went down to the tennis court and were in the middle of a rather lackluster game when Hoddy caught the flash of a camera and ran to the vine-covered fence. The reporter and photographer ran too, but on the other side. Hoddy was helpless, so he tore for the big gates, but couldn't catch the intruders. The pictures were in the papers the next morning, somewhat distorted, but conveying the impression that Meade was anything but a grief-stricken widow.

"You shouldn't have played that game, Meade," Brice told her when he saw the pictures.

"But, Brice, it's like being in prison," Meade said and added, "already."

"My dear child, you are not going to prison. But I can't do much, nobody can do much about the reporters. They earn their living by getting printable news. Why, even I—" He smiled wryly. "As I was coming out of the courthouse in Soundport yesterday I was faced with flashes of lights and questioned about my connection with the Havlock case. Was I really going to defend you? How would it affect my campaign? Would people vote for me if I defended you if you were indicted?"

"If I'm tried for murder. I can't be the cause of your losing the governorship..."

"I'll not lose that. Besides, I owe it to Sam."

Agnes came every day, but even calm Agnes began to show strain; small lines appeared around her beautiful, serene eyes, tiny sharp lines around her mouth. "We have to get started with the campaign. November isn't very far away. But," she told Meade, "you're not to worry about that. Brice and I are sending the children abroad. I've hired a travel-bureau girl to see to them." She sighed. "She may have her hands full."

"Why are you sending them—oh, Agnes! So they won't be associated with me!"

"Nonsense! We decided that it was not fair to subject the children to all the hard work and general tension of a political campaign. When Brice clears you—as he will, Meade, as he will—he'll be very popular."

"Unless people say he got a rich girl off," Meade said sadly. "You know the old saying. Nobody feels sorry for the girl in the Rolls-Royce."

"But you don't have a Rolls-Royce," Agnes said with a laugh which was not quite forced.

"And besides, you're not rich. Yet."

"But they all know. The newspapers..."

"Yes," Agnes said soberly. "Three hundred million dollars. It's like a...a..."

"An albatross," Hoddy said, suddenly appearing. "All the same, I'd just as soon have that kind of albatross."

"No," Meade said, "you wouldn't. If you only knew!"

"We do know," Agnes said. "We understand."

Hoddy escorted Agnes to her car.

He said dourly, returning, "It seems to me the

129

executors, Mr. Bacon for one, are taking their time."

"It seems longer than it really has been," Meade said but couldn't quite believe her own words.

Another day, but no more tennis. Meade began to see the end of the pile of cards that had come with flowers and the stacks of telegrams and letters; she kept on writing, almost the same phrases but what else was there to write except thanks, as gracefully worded as she could manage. Still, there was repetition; there had to be.

Probably every recipient of those notes she was writing would say, or think, "His widow, perhaps she murdered him. All that money."

Andy did not come back and there was no word from him.

Mrs. Dunham did not return and nobody, so far, knew where she had gone. John was still, as Hoddy put it flippantly, among the missing.

She thought of the other summers when she and Sam had spent almost all the time at home. Somehow Sam had got servants, even the previous year; but they were real servants. There was a series of them, at least three couples, as she remembered it. She had barely time to learn their names when they either departed with some of Sam's special port and her own wrist watch, or developed mysterious backaches and couldn't do the work or—and this was an honest reason for leaving—an elderly couple who came to her and said frankly and regretfully that the work was just too much for them and they were sorry. Sam gave them an extra two weeks' pay.

Finally Brice came. Agnes was with him. At her first glance Meade knew what they were going to say before they said it. She said it herself. "The inquiry—"

"Yes," they said. It was to be held at the county courthouse the following day.

130

It was held the next day and the judge formally recommended Meade to the police as the murderer of her husband Samuel Havlock. This time Chief Haggerty did not employ any extralegal powers he might delegate to himself. She was to be imprisoned on the charge of murder.

Ten

Waldo had probably been the most telling witness against her and at the same time the most reluctant and unwilling; he twisted his bony red hands, he looked as if he were going to burst into tears, but he had to answer yes, when next he looked, the vial of the drug they called number 3 dash 256 had disappeared.

There was a great deal of discussion about number 3 dash 256, both its known and unknown properties. Everyone in the stuffy little room, which smelled of floor-cleaning oil and furniture polish, seemed to lean forward, all curiosity, to listen to every word that could be told of the strange new drug. There was far too little. Yet already some of the newspapers were calling it the Numbers murder; which was confusing. As Hoddy remarked, "Sounds as if Sam were mixed up in a racket." Aunt Chrissy leveled a stony gaze on him, and he said no more of that. But the Sam Havlock murder was always featured in big headlines. And his money. That was sometimes exaggerated. Now and then it became a billion.

When asked to do so, Meade sat in a straight oak chair; she answered all the questions she could. Brice had taken her through a kind of rehearsal, but there was really nothing she could say that she hadn't already told the police. Only once was there a variation.

"Were you on good terms with your husband?" the judge asked.

"Yes."

That was true enough. She wanted for someone to say, "But you were planning to ask him for a divorce." Nobody did. Mrs. Dunham must have decided to hold her fire, in order to protect her position so she could continue to ask Meade for money.

It seemed to Meade that nothing else, no smallest fact was left out; Chief Haggerty had made the fullest report. His explanation that he had not felt sufficiently convinced of any evidence proving that Mrs. Havlock had committed murder and thus had not arrested her was accepted as simply as he told it; clearly he was a power in the county as well as in the Cove; what Chief Haggerty did was right.

John's disappearance, and Mrs. Dunham's, were not permitted to be connected in any way with Sam Havlock's murder. Once when Brice tried to bring up the matter of John's disappearance, the judge—old Herman Manders, who was a little deaf and wouldn't look straight at Meade (probably because he hated the obvious task that lay before him, Meade thought)—cut off Brice's mention of John swiftly and curtly. Nothing at all was said of Mrs. Dunham, and if Brice could have

134

pulled a rabbit out of his hat, as Meade hoped almost against hope that he would, he didn't.

However, as she had been advised, it was not a trial, there were not questions leading to her defense; there were only and simply statements of fact.

The inquiry did not last very long; the facts were established as far as possible. The verdict was given. Samuel Havlock had been murdered. It was the judge's recommendation that Meade Forrest Havlock be incarcerated at once. Almost as he spoke, however, an excited kind of scuffle and turmoil suddenly came from the door of the room; men were running down the aisle, approaching the judge. One of them was waving a piece of paper high in his hand as if someone else might seize it. Then Hoddy, his face startlingly white, detached himself from the bustle and commotion around the judge's table and came running to tell her, "Listen—just listen! John did it."

Brice had pulled the rabbit out of the hat after all. Or rather, it developed that a young policeman, delegated to go through Mrs. Dunham's papers to look for clues to her disappearance, had pulled out the rabbit.

The judge held the paper in his hands and stared at it. There was sudden, absolute silence around his chair; it was as if all the men there were fixed in marble, staring and breathless. At last the judge slowly passed the paper to the man nearest him, who read it and passed it solemnly to the next man. It went all around the circle. A newspaperman stood on his tiptoes, stared over somebody's shoulder and then made a dash for the door and, probably, a telephone. The others, mainly armed with cameras, simply remained, staring and waiting. Hoddy whispered to Meade, "They've found a letter. Mrs. Dunham wrote it. It's a blackmail letter. In it she says she saw John put the stuff in Sam's drink and she'll keep her mouth shut if John will pay her."

For Meade the room itself seemed to tilt. Only Agnes' hand on hers was steady and firm. Then the judge himself came from the group of men. He took Meade's hand. "I'm thankful it turned out this way, Mrs. Havlock. Frankly, it was hard for me to believe that you murdered your husband. A policeman has discovered a blackmail letter—"

But Hoddy interrupted, "I told her. But where are Mrs. Dunham and John? Why don't they arrest them?"

The judge did not reply, or if he did, it was not heard because all at once there was a flood of people surrounding Meade. There were flashes and flashes, dazzling to the eyes, from cameras. It was very hot, stifling. "Look this way, please, Mrs. Havlock! This way..." The judge disappeared through the door at the end of the room. But Brice, jubilant and triumphant, pushed his way to Meade. "You are completely exonerated. Free as a bird. A letter was found in Mrs. Dunham's desk—not complete, but enough. She says plainly that she saw John put the poison in Sam's drink and if he pays her she'll keep her mouth shut about it. In short, blackmail."

"I'm not one bit surprised!" said Aunt Chrissy.

Hoddy, white as marble still, said again, "But *where* are Mrs. Dunham and John?"

"Yes," Brice said soberly. "Yes."

Chief Haggerty came over to them, smiling. "All right, now. The judge reversed his decision. You're free. We've got to find Mrs. Dunham, of course."

"And John," said Hoddy. "Why didn't she finish her letter and see to it that John got it?"

Chief Haggerty's pleasant face seemed to close in upon itself. "That we don't know yet. We do know that the note was written on her own typewriter in a kind of office she had fixed up at her house. But there are some questions—"

136

"Questions!" Hoddy cried. "Well, I should think so! Why would she just leave the letter half done and leave her house and her car and vanish into nowhere?"

"Oh, she'll be found. John, too," said the chief and walked away.

But Andy had thought that Mrs. Dunham was murdered. All the way home, riding smoothly back to the beautiful big house, which for a time she had thought she might never see again, Meade could not get Miss Isabel's whispered words out of her mind.

Why had Andy believed Mrs. Dunham was murdered? Where had he gone?

If Mrs. Dunham was murdered, then the obvious suspect would be John. Yet if John had not received the letter, why would he have murdered Mrs. Dunham? If, of course, she was murdered.

There were too many questions. Perhaps Mrs. Dunham had talked directly to John, as she had talked to and threatened Meade herself. But then, why write the letter?

Chief Haggerty's police car followed them.

When they reached the house, the chief sent for Florrie. At the inquest she had been a witness to the fact that Mrs. Havlock herself had prepared her husband's drink; she wore a flowered hat, thin flowery dress and much lipstick and seemed thoroughly to enjoy the limelight, as well as her statement concerning Sam's drink.

They were in Sam's study, all of them, when the chief told Hoddy to call her, and Florrie came in, looking around, half smiling, and disposed herself comfortably in a big leather armchair, kicked off her absurdly high-heeled slippers, removed her flowered hat and sat back as if prepared to enjoy herself. "Actually," she said to the room in general, "I don't know much about John's former life, relatives, anything. You see"—her smile

137

tucked itself in, smugly,—"we weren't really married at all." This, not unnaturally, induced a very thoughtful silence. Florrie herself broke it.

They had thought, she explained airily, it more likely that Madam (again there was a hint, but not quite, of impertinence as she said "Madam") would be more apt to employ them if she thought they were married.

To the obvious fact that they had been sharing the same room not even Aunt Chrissy lifted a haughty eyebrow.

Hoddy however, unexpectedly, reverted to his early upbringing and said, shocked, "Living in sin! Kick her out, Meade."

"Now, now," the chief said, although he struggled to conceal a slight grin as he glanced at Hoddy, "let's not act hastily. Where is John, Florrie?"

"You asked me that. Everybody has asked me that. I haven't the faintest idea. If that's all you want to know..."

The chief said soberly that she must stay there, in the house, and if she heard from John, or had any news whatever about him, she must let him know at once.

Florrie nodded nonchalantly, scooped up her slippers and went out, swinging her hat as if she had scored somewhere, somehow.

There was a long and thoughtful silence. Finally Brice said, "I suppose the main question is, Why didn't Mrs. Dunham finish her letter and see that John received it?"

The chief said slowly, "She may have decided to talk to John..." He sighed and added, "Dangerous. Blackmailers. The letter was just shoved into a drawer of her desk. She has a locked metal filing cabinet. We'll give that a thorough search, easy enough to get it open. We'll have to look up her bank statements or banks, Social Security number, anything at all that will give us a line on where she went and why. You must have had references for her before you hired her, didn't you, Meade?"

"References, yes, of course. Sam saw them. Or Miss Bellamy. He said they were quite satisfactory."

The chief frowned. "Was he exact about such things? Did he really check up on those references?"

"I don't know. To tell you the truth, after the first dinner she cooked for us—that was reference enough."

"But you see," the chief said patiently, "if she set out to blackmail John, she may have tried this scheme in other places where she worked."

She tried to blackmail me, Meade thought, but shook her head. "We ought to have checked thoroughly on the references. Perhaps Sam did. But we were so thankful to get anybody who could cook like that."

"Well, well, do you have any recollection as to what town or city or—anything at all about her previous jobs?"

Meade shook her head. "No, I'm sorry. I should have—"

Agnes said, "We don't! If a famous gangster came along and cooked for us as Mrs. Dunham cooked, we'd keep him. That's simply the way things are, Chief."

"Well, well," the chief said again, "I can see some work ahead for us and some of our neighboring police friends." He went to the door, paused to nod at Meade and say good night, and left.

Agnes sighed. "It'll take months before this thing is settled. Why on earth would Florrie say she was married to John?"

"Probably for the reason she gave," Aunt Chrissy said, as if there was nothing at all about the gyrations of the human race that could astonish her. Brice laughed shortly. "We'd better

139

go, Agnes. Unless there's anything we can do for you," he said to Meade.

She told him no and thanked him. Agnes said thoughtfully, "I think they'll be able to trace Mrs. Dunham's history pretty quickly. As Chief Haggerty said, if she thought of blackmailing John, she probably tried to blackmail other people."

And she did, Meade thought; oh, she did. She said good night to Agnes and Brice. Aunt Chrissy escorted them to the front door. Hoddy and Meade drifted out to the terrace, where, his eyes half closed, he said dreamily, "She didn't try to blackmail you, did she, Meade? Or Sam? Or Aunt Chrissy?"

Aunt Chrissy came out in time to hear that. "Certainly not!" Her eyes flashed. But then she, too, grew very thoughtful. "All the same I can see that, cooking as well as she did, she could get almost any job she wanted. Probably among rich people who could pay if she picked up any blackmail material. Oh, the police will find her and get at the truth. In any event, the whole thing is finished as far as you are concerned, Meade."

Meade watched the little ripples along the Sound coming slowly but steadily in through the reeds where Sam had died. "No," she said at last slowly, "I don't think the whole thing is over for me."

She was right, but it was almost a week before it was known that she was right.

Eleven

Aunt Chrissy had departed kitchenward, saying that that Florrie had better get busy about dinner. After all, life and meals did go on, even if John, who hadn't been her husband at all, had flown the coop. "Not that I *really* thought they were married," Aunt Chrissy had a strong sense of realism. "But in the circumstances...this big house...no servants—it really doesn't seem to matter."

Around ten o'clock Hoddy went down to close the big gates across the driveway. (Later he insisted that he had stopped to take a look at the dogs, who were beginning to like him, he said; at least only one of them had tried to nip him through the heavy wire.) They all went to sleep in a night that was silent, too silent; there was not the sound of a dog even when a car passed along the public

141

highway; as a rule Marcelline gave some kind of protest when this happened. That night there were no protests and when morning came, no dogs at all.

Naturally Waldo telephoned later in a resigned way to say that they were all there; he had put them in kennels about midnight when he heard the growls and snarls of his own dogs, and had gone to find out what was the matter, suspecting that Mrs. Havlock's dogs had come calling again. And he really would appreciate it if Mrs. Havlock would see to it that her dogs were shut up at night.

Hoddy took and relayed the message and declared that everything had been shut up safely when he went out the previous night to check the driveway gate and the kennels.

Florrie, questioned, had turned sullen and said she didn't hear or know anything about it, and if anybody expected her to feed and water those dogs with those great big teeth, they needn't because she wasn't about to do it.

Meade said curtly that she would see to them and immediately went with Hoddy to collect them from an apologetic but indignant Waldo.

That afternoon Miss Isabel arrived, secrecy and prudence written so plainly on her pretty, round face that she might as well have shouted, "I've got a secret!" But when she contrived to get rid of Aunt Chrissy, who could read these signs as clearly as anyone, she told Meade only that she had heard from Andy. She didn't know where he was, but she was to tell Meade that he was accomplishing something, he thought, and he had read the papers, so he knew the outcome of the inquiry. He sent word to Meade to take it easy and wait. It was just about the most exasperating message a man could send to a troubled, frightened young woman.

"But it does sound hopeful, doesn't it?" Miss Isabel said.

"Perhaps he's got a line on Mrs. Dunham," said

Hoddy, who had walked so quietly onto the terrace that Meade was sure he had tiptoed in his sneakers and listened.

Miss Isabel gave a slight start. "Really, Hoddy, it's not polite to eavesdrop."

"I didn't hear anything much." Hoddy draped himself over the balustrade.

"Don't sit on that dreadful railing, Hoddy!" Miss Isabel said, quite sharply for her. "It's too—too reminding." She stopped herself with an abrupt cough, said good-bye to Meade and went to the front door, where Aunt Chrissy came hurriedly to meet her. The two ladies strolled down the driveway together and back again to Miss Isabel's car, parked near the front stairs.

"They're having a good gossip." Hoddy had gone to the hall door, from where he had a view of the front gate and a part of the driveway. "Two old cats—"

"Hoddy!"

"Well, biddies—"

"They've both been very good to you," Meade said sharply.

"You can't deny that they know everything that goes on in the Cove."

"They don't talk about it, though. You've got to admit that."

Hoddy did, grudgingly, by going back to the balustrade and draping himself, his old sneakers, his worn blue jeans and filthy T-shirt in a kind of pretzel snarl. Meade wondered, in some little corner of her mind, when the fashion pendulum would swing to extreme fussiness and cleanliness, dandyism indeed, for young men and hoped it would be soon.

Aunt Chrissy returned after they heard the gentle beat of Miss Isabel's car starting up, but her face was that of an aristocratic clam. Neither Hoddy nor Meade questioned her.

Of course if the two women between them

contrived to find out everything that went on in the Cove, there was still one very important thing they obviously didn't know, and that was the identity, even a surmised identity, of Sam's murderer.

Undoubtedly driven by hunger, Hoddy eventually went to the kitchen and gave a hand to Florrie, who remained oddly pleased with herself. Meade went to help, too. Aunt Chrissy sat in state, waited to be served.

That night again someone apparently entered the house. No one knew of the entry until the next afternoon.

Agnes came in the morning; she was in a rush; she had seen the children off; she thought the travel-agent girl who had been engaged to herd the children through various historical or educational spots in England and France would be able to cope with them. "Now Brice and I will start the campaign touring and speechmaking in earnest instead of these brief overnight trips he's been making. I have some of those clothes that will shake wrinkles out over the bathtub. Also twice as many shirts as Brice thought he'd need. Of course, we'll be back and forth to the Cove constantly. So"—her lovely eyes smiled at Meade—"I'll not be far off, dear Meade. Phone me if you— Any time."

That afternoon Brice, too, came alone in a car, a rather beat-up and shabby car, to say good-bye. "But you can call on me any time. Agnes will keep you informed of our itinerary."

Aunt Chrissy looked at his car. "Do you mean to say you are going to travel in that"—she snorted delicately—"remarkable vehicle?"

Brice looked at it and laughed. From the top of the stairs at the front door, the sun did show up unmercifully the various scars and dents, which probably young Pete could explain. "It'll go. The committee tells me that it makes a better impression on the voters."

The battered vehicle thumped its way down the

drive quite adequately, and Hoddy scampered upstairs to his television set; he had a small one, which he had promised to keep turned low when he felt like watching the late shows. But that afternoon the set wouldn't work at all. He came loping down the stairs. "Meade, can I use the television in Sam's study? Mine won't work."

"May I," his aunt corrected him loftily.

Meade nodded yes but he came back at once, long-faced. "That one won't work either. And there's a ball game I can't miss."

"Try Florrie's. They have one in the pantry," Meade said, looking up from another batch of thank-you notes.

He returned after a while, this time strangely pale, his eyes very bright. "That one won't work either. I found out why. Somebody swiped the tubes out of every single set. Mine and Sam's and Florrie's. She says hers worked yesterday. Mine did too. It must have happened during the night." He stuck his hands through his hair so it stood up wildly over his pale face. "Somebody got into the house again and fixed it so we can't see any television programs."

Meade leaned back in her chair. "But what would anybody in the world want to prevent us from seeing?"

Aunt Chrissy got up and went to the telephone. She dialed firmly; she spoke firmly. "I want Chief Haggerty...When will he be there?...This is urgent...The Havlock place, of course...Well, then tell him we must see him as soon as he can come."

She put down the telephone. "The—I think he called himself the desk sergeant said there's been an accident on the old Cove road. And a rash of vandalism. All the men were busy. They really are short-handed. But Haggerty will see us as soon as he can."

There was a long pause. Finally Hoddy said, "I

don't think this tube theft is exactly vandalism. There's some program tonight that somebody doesn't want us to see. I'll buy another set—okay, Meade? Just a small one..."

She really wished for a moment that she didn't love her brother; there had been days in his youth when she might have shaken some sense into him, she thought with regret. But still, when all was said and done, he was her brother.

"I'll go and buy a television set," he insisted. "We've got to see whatever program someone doesn't want us to see."

Aunt Chrissy kept her head. "If somebody has simply removed the tubes, go and get a repairman, Hoddy. You'd better take enough money to pay for the tubes."

"Sounds reasonable," Hoddy said. "Meade—I mean, money?"

"All right," Meade said. "My black handbag is on the table in my room."

Hoddy took the stairs three at a time. He came down in one crashing tumble. He had some bills in one hand, but he had a piece of writing paper in the other. "Meade! I guess you've seen this. It was in your handbag. But I think you ought to destroy it."

"Destroy?" Meade held out her hand. It was a typewritten line or two, and underneath, a typed signature. "*You know what I told you. You'll know what is best for you. Mrs. Dunham.*"

"What does she mean?" cried Aunt Chrissy. "What on earth—"

Hoddy leaped at the answer. "She saw you with Andy down at the tennis court. She heard every word you said, I'll bet on that. And I'll bet you talked about a divorce from Sam—"

"I said no. I couldn't do that to Sam," Meade said faintly.

There was a long, long pause. Aunt Chrissy turned quietly to stone. Then Hoddy went to the root of it. "We've got to find out who can come and
146

go in the house any time she likes. It's Mrs. Dunham, no doubt of that. But you make a list, Meade, of all the people who had keys to this house, or any way at all of getting in. No, it'll be easier to change the locks. I'll get a locksmith in tomorrow."

But if Hoddy leaped swiftly, Aunt Chrissy emerged from a stone woman and leaped, too. "Did Mrs. Dunham actually try to blackmail you, Meade?"

"Yes." There was nothing else to say.

Aunt Chrissy thrust a distracted hand through her usually neat hair. Hoddy said, "About seeing you with Andy, of course. What did you say? No go?"

"Naturally. Yes. But then she said something like 'Pay me'—"

Hoddy broke in. "Pay me or else. That's what they always say."

"Hoddy!" Aunt Chrissy began.

Hoddy brushed her off quickly. "In all the cops-and-robbers shows. Well, so now what are we going to do? Have you told anybody about this, Meade?"

"Not about this note. I never saw it before. But I told Andy about her threat to me."

There was a long pause during which Aunt Chrissy automatically smoothed her hair back into neatness, but Aunt Chrissy, who would do battle with almost anything, was frightened, Meade thought as if in a nightmare. Hoddy turned practical again. "The first thing to do is make a list of the keys, Meade. Tomorrow I'll have all the locks changed. But right now—somebody doesn't want us to see one of tonight's programs. I'll go for a repairman."

A forgotten question popped into Meade's mind. "Why did you want to borrow more money from Sam? What were you going to do with it?"

Hoddy was airy but frank. "For one thing, I ran out of money. I had just enough to get me back here

147

in August. So I thought and thought and it seemed to me that I might find some small business that needed a little capital. If Sam lent me the capital, then I'd be working for myself, you see. Under my own steam, so to speak. But of course, now I needn't."

"Needn't what?" Meade said sharply. "Look here, Hoddy, if you think I'm ever going to be as generous with money—if I ever really have money—as Sam was, you are very much mistaken. You've got to stand on your own two feet."

Hoddy's eyes widened. "Why, Meade, you wouldn't let your own brother starve!"

"I'd make my brother work for his living. Other men do."

"Sam didn't," said Hoddy, scoring a hit.

The trouble was, Meade thought somberly, that was exactly what Hoddy proposed to do; keep on living on Sam's money.

"I'll get the repairman," Hoddy said. "We'll switch from station to station ..." He ran down the steps and jumped into his car, even more battered than Brice Garnet's.

Florrie, unnoticed, had come into the hall. "I heard what you said. We can check the programs. I'll get the TV magazine."

She brought the guide devoted to television programs and news. The only item that struck any note of familiarity was that of a small local station where Brice was to speak at eight o'clock. At last she gave up with a sigh. "There's nothing left but the late shows, usually old movies." She went away, taking the thick little magazine with her.

Aunt Chrissy pushed her hands over her hair again, smoothing and smoothing. Finally she said, "So Andy really did ask you to divorce Sam? And you said no?"

"I said no then," Meade replied wearily. "Now I'm not so sure. You see, Aunt, it's hard to explain, but I don't think Sam was really in love with me."

148

"But all the things he gave you ... anything you wanted ..."

"Yes, I know. I've thought and thought. But I really can't explain it, Aunt Chrissy. I know that Sam liked me to go about with him. But he was simply not in love with me."

"Then why did he marry you?"

"Because he wanted to, I suppose," Meade said wearily. But then she added with a flash of fire of her own, "And you were all in favor of the marriage, don't forget."

For a moment Aunt Chrissy's haughty face wasn't haughty. She said at last, her voice uneven, "I thought I was advising you for the best, Meade."

"Oh, I know. I understood then and I understand now. It's all right, Aunt Chrissy."

Aunt Chrissy gave herself a little shake, turned away from Meade and picked up a newspaper Hoddy had left. Obviously she was distracting herself, but then, just as obviously she became intensely interested and turned the paper swiftly to the financial section. She had to adjust her eyeglasses to read. Her face turned pale. "Eight more points! Eight and two-thirds to be exact."

"What?" Meade said, confused.

Aunt Chrissy peered at her over the top of the glasses she hated to wear. "Emmeline Company stock, of course. Sam gave me three thousand dollars every year during your marriage. Something about no gift tax. Naturally I used it to buy his own holding company stock. It's been dropping since Sam was—murdered. This makes forty-two and two-thirds altogether. It'll go down still further, I suppose. Didn't you know that?"

"That he gave you money? No. But I'm not surprised."

"He didn't tell me to buy his own stock with it. I just thought it sensible."

There was the sound of a car coming rapidly up the drive. Meade went to the front door as Andy

149

ran up the stairs. She flung the door open.

"Don't touch me," Andy cried. "I'm dusty, dirty and full of—not fleas, I hope, but news. Of a kind. It doesn't get us anywhere."

Aunt Chrissy had followed; she demanded sharply, "Where have you been?"

Andy turned evasive, for he was very tired. "Out of everywhere, into here. Mind if I have a wash and a brush? I've been driving since dawn."

"Andy!" Meade put her arms around him, holding him tight; he caught and held her as if he'd never give her up.

She was vaguely aware of a speedy but erratic rattle on the driveway below, which signaled Hoddy's swift reversal of his car when he met Andy, down the road; he dashed back to the house a few seconds later.

Aunt Chrissy said coldly, "If you must put on such a show, at least go into the study or somewhere so Florrie—"

Andy lifted his head. "Oh, Florrie won't care. She was married to Sam."

Aunt Chrissy sank back slowly against the wall. At last she whispered, "You can't mean that!"

But he did mean it.

Florrie had been listening from the pantry again; she came calmly out into the hall. "Oh, it's true," she said flatly. "Sam married me. Nobody can deny that."

"Good God!"

Hoddy whirled around to Florrie. "I don't believe you."

Florrie shrugged. "Oh, it's true."

"Then you must have been divorced!"

Florrie shrugged nonchalantly.

"But he married my sister! He couldn't have been married to both of you!" Hoddy cried.

Florrie simply turned around, her plump shoulders looking somehow very smug; they could not

150

see her face, but Meade was sure that she was smiling.

Hoddy shouted after her, "But John, what about John? You said you were married to John."

"I also said I wasn't," said Florrie and closed the pantry door.

Twelve

For the first time in her life, red blazing anger surged over Meade. She ran across the hall and flung open the pantry door. "Florrie, come back here at once! You've got to explain all these ...these lies!"

Andy said, rather mildly, behind Meade, "Don't flip your wig, darling. She really was married to him. Briefly, I gather, but supposedly married."

Meade whirled on him. "Divorced?"

"I don't know ... All right, Florrie, come on. You may as well hear what I have to tell."

Florrie came in. She sat down with a stunning air of calm proprietorship. She said to Meade, "You can imagine how I liked being ordered around by you. Florrie, do this—Florrie, do that—Florrie, you must say 'Madam.'"

"Shut up," Andy said mildly but with an

undertone of iron, for Florrie shut up.

"Now then," he went on, "I know about your marriage because I investigated Sam. I even went back to his school days. He was always so impeccable in his behavior that I didn't expect to find anything, but I tried and it seems that when he first went to college he was quite a lad. Went with a lot of kids who were all well-heeled and lazy, and inclined to find odd places to drink. One of these places belonged to your mother, Florrie, and you worked there, serving drinks—"

"I didn't," Florrie flashed.

"Sorry, you did. And one night a justice of the peace was awakened to marry you to Samuel Havlock. He's still alive. I talked to him. He said there was a license all right, and a blood test—how did you manage that, Florrie? Did you just stick a needle into Sam sometime when he was thoroughly drunk and take a sample away? Or did you induce him to go with you to a doctor? Anyway, you got it."

"You're damn right I got it," Florrie said, her face red with anger. "No business of yours."

"No, I really don't see that that part of your little scheme matters much now. The point is, one night you got Sam to go with you to this old fellow, this justice of the peace. He looked up his records and there it was, Samuel Havlock and Florence Cable. And," Andy said very, very deliberately, "the dates."

Florrie looked down at her hands.

"The dates," Andy said, "were the giveaway. You were of age. But Sam's birth date was wrong. In fact, he was not legally of age to marry without parental consent, or, since both his parents were dead, the consent of his legal guardian. So the marriage was not valid."

Florrie jumped to her feet. "Get any law court to say that!"

"Oh, we will," Andy said. "I don't know what

154

you put in his drink—but something. The justice of the peace said it stuck in his mind all this time because the man—Samuel Havlock—seemed a little peculiar, not quite all there. I've inquired of all his old school fellows I could find. One of them was Sam's roommate; he remembers vividly finding Sam collapsed on the porch of his fraternity house on a date which corresponds with your marriage claim. He lugged Sam upstairs and got coffee into him. Then he had to go to class and somebody else apparently came along and got Sam to a hospital. The roommate—I have his name and address if you care to have them—"

"He's a liar!" Florrie said.

"He said that he was puzzled at the time because Sam didn't seem to be drunk; it was more as if he had had some kind of drug and was coming out of it."

Florrie said, "All this is nonsense. I am Sam's wife."

At that instant, Meade was touched by a swift memory of Florrie's referring to Sam once before simply as Sam rather than Mr. Havlock. Suddenly she believed the whole story.

"Sam was not of age," Andy repeated. "He could not have had parental consent and obviously his guardian would never have approved. So the marriage was void. His marriage to Meade, I mean Mrs. Havlock, will be determined to have been perfectly legal. Sam had to have a clean slate for his public and private life. But he was afraid you would publish your version of all this. Did you follow his career, get your clutches in him—"

"Not clutches," Florrie cried. "Never! He married me!"

"—and threaten him?" Andy went on. "Force him to give you some kind of income? But naturally, knowing that you had no legal claim, you accepted his offer of a job for you and John and money. Cash, I expect."

"He paid them in cash," Meade said wearily.

"By the way, who is John? What is he?"

Florrie hesitated for a moment. Then she said flatly, "I'm not going to say a word until I consult a good lawyer. You can't do me out of my claim to Sam's money. Three hundred million dollars. All to his wife." This time she walked back to the pantry, but rather slowly and thoughtfully.

Aunt Chrissy, who had sunk straight down on the floor with her handsome head leaning back against the wall and her pretty and beautifully shod feet stuck out in front of her, began slowly to pull herself up; once upright, she gave herself a little shake like a bird smoothing its feathers and said in a quiet but businesslike way, "How much should we give her to pay her off?"

Meade said slowly, "Aunt Chrissy, if all this is true, she should have some money..."

"If it was an illegal marriage, then it was no marriage at all," Aunt Chrissy said.

"Then why do you want to pay her off?" Hoddy asked.

"Why, who wants a story like that noised around?" Aunt Chrissy snapped.

Hoddy had one of his flashes of perception. "Sam couldn't have gone on his way as an outstanding citizen and philanthropist and general do-gooder with that little—"

"Hoddy!" his aunt flashed warningly.

"I was only going to say, with that little story hanging on his coattails. Why, he's got a standing in this state, he's got— Good heavens, do you suppose he had a political future in mind? I never thought of it before, but good Lord, how he gave! How he talked at every dogfight! How he gave, gave, gave, to public enterprises." He turned to Meade. "Did he ever say anything about running for office for...oh, anything?"

"No, never. Not Sam."

"Then why did he give away so much money? He must have expected some kind of return for it." Hoddy could reason when he chose to.

"No, Hoddy. I think you're wrong. Sam merely felt the responsibility his father had had, his grandfather had had. None of them was interested in politics. They just wanted to—"

"—share the wealth," Hoddy said sarcastically. "I don't believe it."

Aunt Chrissy took Meade's side. "Hoddy, I think you are behaving in a most unbecoming manner! Didn't he give you money? Did he ever expect even to get it back?"

Hoddy had the grace to flush a little.

But Meade was thinking hard. If Sam had believed his marriage to Florrie was illegal, then he had had a perfect legal right to marry her, Meade. But he'd have made sure of it; he'd have done something about it. He'd have got legal advice, even a divorce, some kind of divorce, any kind of divorce, if he thought it advisable. He'd have made everything safe before he married Meade. Yet he *had* apparently looked for Florrie; he *had* engaged her and John at probably a preposterously generous wage. It just *could* be that he wanted to keep Florrie's mouth shut because Florrie did have a certain hold on him; the story itself was not a pretty one, not one that agreed with the public image of Sam. Indeed, Meade couldn't imagine Sam doing anything at all that would bring adverse criticism on him. He always pleased everybody almost as if it were important to him. It was a politician's game, she knew. Yet surely, if Sam had had any political aspirations, he would have told her, he would have asked her to help him.

Perhaps that was why he had urged her to try to remember names and faces.

There was a long silence. Aunt Chrissy did move at last in a reasonably stately fashion to a chair.

157

Hoddy murmured something about Florrie's getting dinner for them. "I don't suppose she will ... If she thinks she's the lady of the house."

"Oh, I can cook," Meade said absently. "And you can help me, Hoddy."

"Well, there was something I was about to do ..."

Andy sat down. He said soberly, "None of you seems to have given all this information any particular significance. I mean—"

"Florrie!" Hoddy gasped. "She had the opportunity to put that stuff in Sam's drink, and she had a motive, a claim, she thought, to Sam's money." He paused and added cheerfully, "There are certainly two more likely suspects!"

There was a long silence and then all at once a babble; everyone speaking at once. After some effort, silencing Aunt Chrissy, silencing Hoddy, Meade said firmly that she didn't believe Florrie would have murdered Sam, no matter what claim she thought she might have or what threat she might cast upon Sam's standing as a responsible, outstanding citizen. "And besides, she hates the dogs. I don't think she was ever in Waldo's office! How could she have known of this stuff? Who would have told her?"

"But she did have the opportunity. She certainly had a motive because she clearly believes she's got a claim to his money," Aunt Chrissy said. "All the same, I think I agree with you, Meade. I don't think she'd have the *sense* to do this! I mean—"

"We know perfectly well what you mean," Hoddy broke in. "But all the same, the police—"

"Oh, the police know about it. I stopped to see Chief Haggerty," Andy said. "First, Meade, you'll have to talk to Sam's lawyer about this. Find out just how his will was worded. If he left his money merely to his wife, there could be a fracas. If he willed it to you by name, then Florrie can't do much."

"Three hundred million," Hoddy said mournfully.

"Cheer up," Andy said briefly. "It's still there, I hope. When do you want to talk to the lawyer, Meade?"

"Now, I suppose. Yes."

All of them stood at her elbow beside the telephone, but Mr. Bacon had left the office, indeed the entire office except for one lingering file clerk, was closed.

"Do it tomorrow, then," Andy said. "Meantime it wouldn't hurt to get Brice's opinion about all this. Let's call him."

"He's speaking somewhere tonight," Meade said.

Hoddy leaped up from the armchair he had dropped into as if stricken. "The tubes!" He galloped for the door and down the stairs. In a second it seemed they heard the rattle of his old car starting. Andy said, puzzled, "What tubes?"

Meade explained. Andy listened, his face a blank. "So someone doesn't want you to see some show. Leaves a wide margin. How many people have a key to the house, Meade?"

"I don't know honestly. I meant to make a sort of list but—Andy, it's been so many years, people coming and going. I don't think anybody could make such a list."

"Didn't Sam ever have new locks put in?"

"No, at least I don't think so. It's always been so safe here. I suppose we just didn't think of it. But we are having new locks. Hoddy will get the locksmith in the morning."

"It may be important," Andy said gravely.

Florrie came out of the pantry. "I may as well get your dinner for you."

"Oh—well, thank you," Meade said helplessly and added, as helplessly, "I'll help you."

Regardless of everything, this woman had once thought herself Sam's wife. Certainly the whole

159

thing must have happened the way Andy told it, yet Florrie had an excuse to feel not only rejected but cheated out of her inheritance. However, if the marriage was not legal...

Andy might have been reading her thoughts. He said to Florrie kindly and quietly, "We'll get a lawyer, Florrie. You get your lawyer too. We'll try to straighten this out."

"The money is mine," Florrie said. "I listened at the door. I heard that man, that executor or whatever he was, say Sam left money to his wife. Well, I'm that wife—"

"So am I," Meade said, unexpectedly overtaken by a fighting spirit. Andy gave her an approving look.

"Until we can get some firm legal advice—" he began, but Florrie interrupted, "I'll sue! See if I don't! and I'll bet you anything that's what my lawyer will tell me to do." With which she marched off to the pantry again.

"And she *will* sue," Aunt Chrissy said sourly. "That's what makes lawyers rich."

"Not always," Andy said. "Now, Miss Chrissy, let's give this some time. See what happens."

Aunt Chrissy gave him a scorching look. "Opportunity...motive—"

"But possibly not the means," Andy said. "Of course they'll inquire of Waldo, try to find out if Florrie ever went near his place—"

"Or John," Aunt Chrissy said darkly. "John had the opportunity. Florrie could have promised him a share in the money she expected to get. And Mrs. Dunham's letter to John may have been based on fact!"

Andy sighed. "I know, I know. So does Chief Haggerty. But believe me, nothing, just nothing at all can be settled tonight, this minute."

But it was settled, or some of it, at ten o'clock. Hoddy had returned, tubeless and furious, since

160

the only two repair shops were closed by the time he reached them. He said crossly that he couldn't think of anybody he could borrow from and sat brooding like a disconsolate crow with a curly wig.

Florrie had served the dinner, scorning Meade's offer to help. Then Andy helped Florrie carry out the dishes, and Meade could hear them talking briefly while they rinsed the plates and put them in the dishwasher. It wouldn't have hurt her to help, too, she thought with not the slightest twinge of conscience. She could clearly imagine Sam, a young Sam, kept at home with private tutors until he was let off the leash and sent away from home, falling into what was nothing less than a trap and going through a wedding ceremony—"as if he had been drugged." Hadn't Andy said that? And Sam himself underage.

Yet he had hired Florrie; perhaps he felt sorry for her; perhaps he wasn't trying to cover his early mistake at all.

Aunt Chrissy had been thinking too. "Tomorrow, we've got to get hold of Mr. Bacon and tell him about Florrie. Ask how Sam's will is worded." She paused and added, "The appraisers must examine his safe-deposit box. He might have had a number of safe-deposit boxes. Well," she said, cheering up slightly, "they'll find them. *Somebody* will have a record."

The appraisers would find all the jewels, Meade thought. The jewels he had given her to wear—she stopped abruptly and revised her own thought—the jewels he had lent her to wear! But he had said once that he would have his mother's jewels reset in a modern way—for her, he had said.

It struck her again that in fact she knew very little of Sam's mental reactions; he was never an eager conversationalist; the things they talked of always seemed curiously impersonal.

Perhaps her own inward thoughts and feelings

161

were so engrossed with Andy that she too had been impersonal, keeping all talk on an easy, superficial level, as Sam had done.

He hadn't mentioned Florrie until he came to tell her he had hired Florrie and John to work for them that summer. There had not been the slightest hint in his manner that he had once supposed Florrie to be his wife. A good fat salary, and Florrie would keep her mouth shut. Yet if Florrie felt she had a real claim, would she have consented to this arrangement?

Florrie—or Florrie and John, acting together—*did* have the opportunity to introduce that drug into Sam's drink, and might have believed themselves to have a motive—Florrie's inheritance from Sam if it meant only a widow's third of his estate. On the other hand, wouldn't they have known that they would have the first and very obvious suspects? So perhaps that was why John had taken himself off, scared, she knew. Florrie, being of sterner stuff, had decided to brazen it out.

But surely Waldo would know if either of them had ever seen or heard of a drug which was known to so limited a number of people. It wasn't as if there had been any similar cases in, say, the newspapers; it wasn't as if there had been, to her knowledge, any widespread recognition of its lethal effect. Even the men at the laboratory had been uncertain, trying to analyze its properties and so far failing to agree upon any certain lethal qualities.

No. She didn't think Florrie, or John, had murdered Sam, even if they did have opportunity and motive. She wished that Sam had told her something of that early marriage, which was really no marriage, when he brought Florrie and John to work in the house. She tried to deny any unwelcome little spear of cruel reflection, but the fact was she had scarcely known her husband.

162

She was sitting on the terrace—remembering Sam balancing on the balustrade, sipping the drink which she had prepared for him and which was also loaded with the barely identifiable poison—when Hoddy, who had gone into the house, came bursting out again. "It's John and Mrs. Dunham...on television! Miss Isabel saw them—"

Both Aunt Chrissy and Meade ran to the telephone but Meade by an adroit swerve got there first.

"It was John and that Mrs. Dunham! I was watching an old movie," Miss Isabel said, "and there they were, in the same cast. If you'll hurry you can see the film. It's still on—"

"We can't; somebody took all the tubes out of our television sets. Oh, Miss Isabel, go back and watch it and—"

Andy took the phone from her hand. "Watch it through and see if their names are listed at the end of the movie, and write down the name of the movie and the producer."

Aunt Chrissy went like a well-fed pigeon straight for the kitchen. "Florrie, come out here! Was John ever in the movies?"

Florrie emerged with her hair done up in huge rollers and a brilliantly flowered dressing gown floating around her. She grasped the situation at once, however. "Somebody saw him on television."

Andy replied, "Miss Isabel. She's watching now to get all the information she can."

Florrie did not look at all perturbed. "I always thought he was hiding something—that is, nothing criminal of course but just—well, he never told me anything much of himself. Didn't seem to want to talk about anything in his past."

Aunt Chrissy flew to attack. "Naturally not, if he thought just possibly he'd made a bigamous marriage."

"Oh, but he didn't! I never told him about Sam."

163

Aunt Chrissy's mouth fell open. Andy said slowly, "Do you mean to say that John never knew why you took the job here?"

"None of his business," said Florrie airily. She added quickly, though, "But he had his share of the money Sam paid me—I mean us."

I will not like her, Meade told herself; I will not. Yet a tiny seed of something like pity, like compassion had planted itself within her awareness; the woman had had a hard life, she was making the best of what she could do, she was a fighter.

Andy persisted. "But you knew that if you were actually still legally married, it would be bigamy to marry another man."

Florrie was not to be frightened, not even upset; she adjusted a curler which seemed to pull too hard. "I thought you wanted to let the law settle that," she said and went back through the pantry, up the back stairs to the room she and John had shared.

There was a long silence. At last Andy went to the telephone receiver, which was still hanging by its cord, and very thoughtfully replaced it. "Of course," he said flatly, returning, "if Mrs. Dunham knew John before, she may have known something of his past which he preferred to keep a secret. It would explain her note to him. But it doesn't explain why she never gave it to him."

"She told him," Hoddy said. "That's it. She decided not to send the letter she started but to talk to him instead. So she told him and threatened to blackmail him. Yes, that was exactly what happened. So John was scared—got away. I wonder," Hoddy said thoughtfully, "what he had done. He never struck me as having much in the way of—oh, strength of mind or muscle to do anything very—very"—he hesitated and airily invented a word—"blackmailable. On the other

164

hand, he may have murdered her."

Nobody had heard the police car arrive. Nobody had heard Chief Haggerty enter the hall or ring the bell, if he did, but all at once he was simply there, a look on his face which stopped their voices; even, Meade thought vaguely, her heart had stopped beating.

"Mrs. Dunham's been found," said Chief Haggerty. He took out a handkerchief and wiped his face.

After a moment Andy said, "Where?"

Hoddy began to understand. "You don't mean...but I just now said—" he started and the chief said, "You'd better sit down, Meade, you and your aunt. This isn't very nice."

"Where was she?" Andy asked again.

"In the Sound. Strangled. Rocks tied up in a sack and fastened to her. Boys out fishing with night crawlers snagged some of the sack, and they tugged her up far enough to see. One of them ran for his father. Another showed good sense and ran for me. And then," the chief said with a hint of anticlimax, "he got sick."

"What—" Hoddy began.

The chief gave him one look. "I went myself. Took some of my boys with me. No doubt it's Mrs. Dunham. Some change, of course. I'd say she's been there for several days. However, the medical examiner will be able to tell us more exactly about that."

Bad things can happen to blackmailers; when, where had someone said that, Meade thought. Had she only thought it herself? But this...oh, this...

The chief said, as if merely reciting something which was quite impersonal, meant no more to him than the license numbers of a speeding car, "She was wearing a black dress. No coat. Strangled with a scarf which we think was her own. I showed it to her neighbor. The neighbor didn't see her

165

drive up to her house that night. It was only the next morning that she noticed the car was still outside and the lights on in the house." He was merely reciting facts; his voice was uneven and very, very tired. "So it looks as if somebody maybe got into the car with her, strangled her, drove the car out to that rocky point, you know, we call it Tar Point, nobody knows why, but you can get down close to the Sound there. He must have been prepared with a sack; he could have got plenty of stones around the point."

"He?" said Aunt Chrissy.

"Well, Mrs. Dunham wasn't really heavy for a man to carry, and I suppose a strong determined woman could have dragged her out of the car and into the water. It seems likely that somebody made some kind of excuse and got into her car with her and—simply strangled her with her scarf. Dumped the body at Tar point and brought the car back. My boys are going over the car and house now for fingerprints," he added as if that would be an obvious part of the routine, as indeed it was. "Also inquiring of the neighbors. So far nobody saw anyone with her. But it would be a very easy murder if her murderer knew about pressure points." As if by accident, Meade thought, his gaze fastened upon Aunt Chrissy.

It wasn't by accident, for Aunt Chrissy, white as chalk said, "You darn fool, Haggerty! You know I've always taken an interest in the Red Cross. I know all about pressure points and—and things like that."

"Well," the chief said wearily, "that doesn't mean you killed her, Miss Chrissy. But somebody did. Have you heard anything about that man of yours, that actor you hired—John? Where's Florrie?"

"I'm here," Florrie said, emerging, curlers and all, from the gloom of the stairway. "I listened to it all. You've heard. You know I was married to Sam.

I don't think John could have killed her. He didn't have the g—I mean, the—"

Hoddy said, "If you mean the guts to kill her, say so. Nothing can shock us now."

Aunt Chrissy might not have heard the little exchange which at one time would have ended with a smart box on the ear for Hoddy. Chief Haggerty said carefully, "Now, Florrie—I mean..." He looked at Meade. "As soon as Andy came and told me the whole story of Sam Havlock's marriage—his first marriage, I mean, to this Florrie—I take it he has told you."

Andy nodded. "The chief said he'll try to keep it out of the newspapers. Unless of course at some future time—if Florrie makes trouble, lawyers, what not—it will have to be told."

It was true, of course. Aunt Chrissy said coolly, "*Why* can't we settle with Florrie? Why can't we give her enough money—"

She had forgotten that Florrie, curlers sticking out, had ears that were sticking out, too. "Oh no, you don't!" she cried. "I'll have my rights." And she flounced into the pantry.

Andy said, "We—or rather my cousin Isabel told us that Mrs. Dunham was once an actress and played in a movie Miss Isabel was watching. And John was in it too."

The chief sighed. "That may be a help. I'll check with Miss Isabel and get Florrie down at the police station in the morning. She's stubborn now. She'll have a chance to think things over by then."

Aunt Chrissy said suddenly, "You'd better get a good night's sleep first, Chief."

He gave her one tired yet friendly glance and simply trudged down the hall and out the door; they could hear his footsteps on the iron steps. Andy murmured something and went after him. Presently they heard the two cars start up and travel down the driveway.

"So that," said Aunt Chrissy at last, "is the end of Mrs. Dunham."

But she was mistaken; it was not entirely the end of Mrs. Dunham.

Thirteen

"'The evil that men do lives after them; the good is oft interred with their bones.'" It was Hoddy who gloomily quoted it.

Far into the night the quotation nagged at Meade; she couldn't keep away from it; it was like pushing at an aching tooth. It didn't matter; it was only a quotation Hoddy had come out with, unexpectedly as he did many things, but in the end she got into dressing gown and slippers, and turning on lights as she went, reached Sam's study, where books were in neat ranks along the wall, and found it. Of course Hoddy had quoted correctly from *Julius Caesar*. What did it matter except to give her some question she could answer?

She was huddled down in a chair with the copy of *Julius Caesar* open on her lap when Andy came back. He touched the bell, the electric bell, very softly, almost as if he hoped she might be waiting for him—as she was, she thought dimly. Her search for the exact quotation had been merely an excuse to wait and listen for Andy. She thought he had said something like "I'll be back" as he followed the chief.

Almost at once, Aunt Chrissy had retired to her own room, unsuccessfully shielding a bottle of Southern Comfort under her arm. And a good idea, Meade had thought. She had too clear an understanding of her aunt's strong character to harbor the notion that she might be overtaken by sudden alcoholism. Leprosy, perhaps. Bubonic plague, possibly. But alcoholism, never.

She ran to the door and flung it open.

Andy came in but said crossly, "You ought to have asked who it was. My God, Meade—oh, never mind."

"Where...what..."

"Come on. Let's go into the study. No need to stand out here in the hall." He settled himself down on the arm of her chair, and suddenly looking down very seriously into her eyes, took her chin with his hand, lifted it and kissed her. "You know," he said, half laughing, "I honestly can't believe you were ever Sam's wife. But legally I am sure you were. Now then—I went with Chief Haggerty to the police station. Identified what I could." He turned rather gray-white. "A body changes in water; that is—now, Meade, stop it. You'll be having hysterics and I'll have to call Aunt Chrissy."

She choked with something like a giggle on that, but it stopped her shivering. "You can't. She's half drunk by now."

"Oh, really?" Andy said casually. "Well, the chief knew no more than he had told us. That is, apparently he knew no more. Actually I got the idea that he's had men all around the neighboring towns and police connections in New York trying

170

to find out anything they can about Sam. The chief said that Mr. Bacon came up with Sam's main bank, seems he used several just for checking accounts, convenience, that's all, but he had a very big safe-deposit box in one bank. The appraisers will get into it soon, with the lawyers, and the chief said, almost as an afterthought, that if we can find Sam's keys to the box, it will be a help. Otherwise they'll have to drill through—"

She nodded. "They were in his desk. Here, I know where ..."

It wasn't a secret drawer; it was merely a drawer that could be pulled not all the way out, leaving a space behind it; she groped around in the dusty space and found two keys, both still in a little red envelope.

"He should have divided them," Andy said absently, taking the keys. "Then if you lose one, you still have the other. If you lose them both, it costs like the devil to drill into the box. Not that that would bother Sam. I have a feeling this was not his only safe-deposit box. Did he use this one very much?"

"I don't know, Andy. These are the only keys I know about. When we were in New York he always put the jewels I wore in this safe-deposit box, just as soon as I took them off. He said there was no use getting my head bumped in."

"Sensible," Andy said dryly. After a moment he said, "Didn't you have the slightest feeling of possession about the jewelry?"

"Why, I don't know. I don't think I ever thought of it."

Suddenly, for no reason she could understand, he kissed her again, lovingly, warmly and possessively. "Now," he said briskly, "we'll get this business of Florrie straightened out. I got hold of Brice."

"He's gone—"

"He was asleep in his hotel. The political

171

meeting was over long ago. He's driving back here now. It's only about fifty miles. I want to talk to him about this Florrie marriage. I rather think he knows about it. The marriage was void. No question of that. But she might claim—oh, something or other, that she was defrauded, any old thing. Do you care much—very much, I mean—about the money?"

"Anybody would care about money, I suppose," Meade said honestly. "Of course I must care, but not all that much."

"After the luxuries of the life Sam gave you for three years you must be pretty well accustomed to money—I mean, large money."

"Not caring what anything cost? Yes. I suppose I enjoyed it."

"You know damn well you did. I can't give you anything like that."

Meade shot up from her chair. "Now, Andy, we're not going to have any nonsense about my money, if I have any, or your money or—"

The doorbell could not have rung at a more inappropriate time. Andy muttered unusual swear-words—probably learned in his travels, Meade thought forgivingly as he went to open the door. Agnes and Brice came in. Both were pale and hurried and had obviously been quarreling. Agnes flung off her cashmere coat, sat down, all sleek and polished as if she'd not been hurtled out of bed on such an errand, and said, not coolly, but very hotly, not like Agnes, "I told Brice he ought to have told you the whole truth!"

"All right, Agnes. All right! But I didn't recognize Florrie. I'd never seen her! Florrie—I might have remembered her name was Florence something, but I didn't! It never occurred to me."

Brice was angry too. But he settled down in a chair, brushed his rather ruffled hair from his neat lawyer's face and said, "Of course I knew all about this illegal marriage, Meade. The guy that pulled

172

Sam into the house that night called me. When Sam came to his senses he told me what he could remember of the situation. I didn't know what to do. I did know that the girl had contrived this marriage. Sam remembered just enough to give me an idea of what had happened.

"Now, wait. That's not the whole story. Remember I was young, just finishing law school. I made the mistake of not getting advice from an experienced man, so I did get a divorce for Sam. A kind of divorce," Brice said miserably. "It was a way out, I thought, and so advised Sam. Sam felt perfectly free to make a real marriage, a legal marriage at any time. He paid something to the girl, this Florrie; I couldn't stop that. Indeed, it made it easier all around. So I sent Sam off to Mexico. I didn't know, like a dolt, that in our state the so-called marriage was void because of Sam's being underage and without his guardian's consent. If I hadn't been so upset and flurried, I'd have taken time, I'm sure. I'd have done what I would know enough to do now—simply tell Sam to forget it, pay the girl something if he wanted to, but tell her that it was no marriage at all. So you see how I've felt about it. I only hoped that nothing of the stupid story would ever come out. Sam was so prominent; the newspapers would have loved it. Sam had, I told you, gone off to Mexico and gone through divorce proceedings there without informing the girl, and before I had the sense to inquire and consult somebody with experience. Sam's trip to Mexico was entirely unnecessary. However—" Brice paused thoughtfully—"I thought it had settled everything thoroughly in the girl's mind. Sam never told me that he had employed her. He wouldn't have told me. I would have been appalled."

"You wouldn't have opposed Sam," Agnes said severely.

Brice shrugged. "Perhaps not. He was very

173

helpful to me. He made a splendid nominating speech and he was doing all the political chores, getting the pols on my side, talking, giving—he was always giving." He sighed. "That's all."

"It isn't all," Agnes said. "How did that girl manage the marriage?"

"I'm not sure! But apparently she turned up with Sam, a license, blood tests, everything, at the office of a justice of peace. She's nobody to fool around with, that girl. Maybe she murdered Mrs. Dunham simply because Mrs. Dunham had something on her—this divorce perhaps. Mrs. Dunham turned out to be a blackmailer. Have they got hold of any of the other people she worked for, Andy?"

Andy sighed. "I don't know. Chief Haggerty said they were working on it, but it's difficult, he said, and I can understand it. I mean, going to see somebody and saying, 'Oh, by the way, is there some dark secret in your past that this Mrs. Dunham blackmailed you about?' Not likely to get a very happy admission, is it?"

"But see here, what about her bank account? If she was stowing away blackmail money, she must have put it somewhere."

"There's some trouble there, too. Best Haggerty can figure out is that she simply kept a safe-deposit box somewhere and kept all her money in it—cash, if you please," Andy said dryly. "She wouldn't want to take checks which could be stopped or at worst could entangle her in a trial for blackmail, so she probably stuffed cash away in some safe-deposit box. But so far, the chief said, they haven't found any clue as to what bank.

"She paid her rent promptly, in cash, and was, in the owner's words, a good and reliable tenant. She was new here, that's true, but she may have exhausted previous fields of activity. In any event," Andy went on, "they're working on it. Even getting help from New York City police, help from all the banks in this vicinity too. But she must have had a short acting career years ago. At least I say 'short' because I don't remember ever seeing her in a movie and neither does my cousin Isabel, and Isabel lives by the television. When she was younger, she lived by going to the theater. She's a walking encyclopedia of stage names."

"And Florrie, what does she say?"

"Turned stubborn. The chief says he'll question her tomorrow more thoroughly and a little more toughly, I'd guess. However, she may know very little of John."

"She may also know where he is," Brice said but not very hopefully. "Although if he murdered Mrs. Dunham, he'll take good care to keep hidden. Use another name. He was an actor. He might even use a disguise. Oh, I don't mean false whiskers," Brice said as Andy gave an exasperated, "Come on, Brice!"

"I mean, something ... subtle," Brice went on. "But that would change him." He paused, frowning, thinking hard. "Now, I gather, Meade, that you want to know what, if any, kind of claim Florrie could make. My first opinion is that she has no basis of claim whatever. I've never had another case like this but I still"—he smiled rather weakly—"have my own law library. However, just now I'd say that if she does propose to make any kind of stir—any kind of claim some shabby lawyer can think up—the best thing would be for you to pay her off. Simplest. But you'll consult Sam's legal firm and the executors of his will."

Andy said quietly, "Wouldn't Meade have to go on paying her off if she once started it? It would be very much like yielding to the first blackmail demand, wouldn't it?"

"Yes, it might be. But after a time this whole tragic affair will be forgotten, people do forget, the public is fickle that way, fortunately sometimes."

"But she's very poor," Meade said.

Andy smiled at her, understanding.

Brice understood too. "All right. Go ahead and give her something. But you can't make any move at all, Meade, until after the whole business of proving the will. With an estate like Sam's, every penny has to be scrutinized, every transaction."

"I do see that," Meade said. "But if Florrie goes to a lawyer—"

"We'll cross that bridge when we come to it," Brice said.

Agnes rose and said firmly, "Will you come with me, Meade? I want to talk to you alone."

"All right," Brice said with a sigh, "but it's no good raking over all that ancient history."

"It's not so ancient that I can't remember it," Agnes said flatly and took Meade by the hand.

"Now then," Agnes said, once they were in the big living room and the door was closed, "didn't Sam ever tell you that I was once engaged to him?"

"You and Sam?"

Agnes nodded. "Brice doesn't really care if I talk about it. Not that I ever do. It *is* ancient history, but it might explain something to you. I don't know, perhaps I'm doing the wrong thing. But you see . . . I'll be frank—did you ever feel really close to Sam?"

"Why, I was his wife! I mean, I . . ." Meade took a deep breath. Agnes' beautiful eyes, calm even now, seemed to force her to tell the truth. "No," said Meade.

"Was he in love with you?"

Again the candid gaze demanded the truth.

"No. I didn't realize it. But that summer we married—I can't explain . . ."

"You needn't," Agnes said. "I can put two and two together. Andy had left you. Your father was dead. You had no money. Your Aunt Chrissy was beside herself. Sam came along. Sam wanted a wife, and a wife he knew all about, had known since she was a child. He knew you weren't after him for his money—too many women had been!"

176

"But, Agnes, why didn't you marry him?"

"I'll tell you." Agnes looked down at her hands for a long time. "I'm not so sure I could make anybody else understand. I believe you can understand. You see, Sam was one of those people who cannot love. No, I mean it. It's as if that—call it ability—has been left out of their make-up. He loved himself, but that was an exclusive love. He really, honestly couldn't love anybody else."

Meade's mouth opened and shut. I'm gasping like a fish, she thought, and said quite clearly and surprisingly, "How did you know that?"

"I don't know. Instinct. Something. Sam made a great fuss over me, he made all the gestures, but all at once I just knew that he was not in love with me. That's all. So I didn't give a hoot—well," she confessed, "not much of a hoot, anyway—about his money. I did think that over. But I was young, and money, no kind of money would make up for being in love with a man who was not in love with me. And as soon as I saw that clearly, no dodging it, I told Sam it was no go. And he didn't mind."

"Not mind, not mind at all?"

"Not a single bit. Truly. He even made me keep the ring he had given me. This one." She held up her hand with its large, lovely emerald. "Told me to keep it with his good wishes. Believe it or not, that's what happened."

After a short pause Meade said, "Yes. I believe you. Sam always liked emeralds. His favorite stone."

"I kept it and I wore it, but on the other finger. As you see, still do. Brice doesn't care, and it's so beautiful! Sam himself introduced me to Brice and I fell in love. Real love," Agnes said softly. "Brice, and my children—oh, Meade, I have felt so sorry for you in your marriage."

"It had to come to an end sometime, I suppose," Meade said slowly. "But I hadn't thought of marriage ever ending. I just thought—there I was,

Sam's wife, nothing could change it. I'd never see Andy again, so it didn't matter. And Sam kept things so busy, you know, always on the go. Agnes! Didn't Brice tell you about his first marriage ever?"

"Not till tonight. After Andy phoned him. Not a word. But Florrie—they'll get that straightened out. Everything takes time," Agnes said almost savagely. She leaned forward. "Meade, did it ever occur to you that maybe somebody was jealous of Sam?"

"Who?" Meade said blankly. "No, no! You don't mean Andy?"

"I don't mean Andy. He might want to kill, but he wouldn't do it that way. No, I was thinking of somebody this political setup, this race for governorship, might affect so badly if Brice is elected that he thought the safest thing was to get rid of Sam."

"But Brice is the one—"

"I know, but Sam was behind him. Sam's influence—" Agnes looked suddenly defeated. "Oh, it's a wild notion, of course. If somebody who ought to go to jail and Sam knew ought to go to jail, I mean somebody Brice has, or will have when elected, the power to send to jail—well, somebody like John. Maybe."

"You mean, John was involved in some illegal activity and Sam guessed it, so John killed Sam to prevent him from helping Brice—no, Agnes. It's too far-fetched."

"I suppose so. All the same, in politics a lot of curious things develop. As a matter of fact, sometimes I wondered if Sam had some political ambition. Had he?"

"Why, I don't know. He never said so."

"But he did rally around every public undertaking with speeches and money. I thought maybe he wanted to be a congressman."

178

"He never said so."

"No? Well, I may be mistaken. But, you see, his helping Brice so constantly brought him very much before the public eye, too. However, I don't think Sam would have been content with anything less than United States senator. Brice, as governor of his home state, could have helped Sam. And Brice is certainly indebted to Sam. I may be all wrong. Yes, Brice?"

Brice had opened the door; he went to Agnes and put his arm around her; she leaned back against his shoulder, and Meade thought, Why, I never did that with Sam. I never felt peace and confidence; I don't think I ever felt anything; I only wanted Andy.

Brice said, "I suppose you told Meade about your own engagement to Sam."

Agnes nodded.

"All right, then. I don't see what good it does. Don't see any harm either. It's very late, Agnes."

It was indeed very late; the little French clock on the mantel struck three. Agnes kissed Meade lightly on her cheek and went away with her arm linked through Brice's arm.

How wise of Agnes, years ago, to understand Sam. He really couldn't love anybody! He pretended; he must have recognized his own infirmity; it was like being born with some curious twist of—not mind or body, but . . . Meade hunted for a word and found it—soul.

But he gave. He was generous. He wanted people to like him. Political ambition? She supposed it was possible, but she had had no hint of it from Sam.

Andy came to her as she sat there thinking hard. "I'm going now, Meade. Don't dwell on all this. You see, Sam wanted people to like *him*." He might have read Meade's thoughts, but she put a different interpretation on them. "There are people

179

like that. They do, they give if it's easy, but not *for* somebody, only to be liked ... The skies may be brighter tomorrow."

More likely darker, Meade thought, even as she clung to him for a moment and then found her way upstairs. Hoddy heard her, stuck his head out of his room, yawned, said, "High time you were going to bed," and shut the door again.

It was just as well that Hoddy with his stubborn digging at facts hadn't heard the long conversations.

Aunt Chrissy's door remained uncompromisingly closed. However, there was a delicate yet high and penetrating snore coming from behind its neatly waxed panels. Sleeping it off, Meade thought with a quiver of humor.

There was nothing humorous the next morning.

It was gray and very still; not a leaf moved. Florrie took off after a telephone call, and a very stern one, Meade thought likely, from the chief of police. She went by taxi; defiant again in high heels and a transparent, oily-looking raincoat over her flowered dress, and her face set and sullen.

Aunt Chrissy came down late, and without any apology or explanation at all, drank at least a quart of tea. She then sighed and said, "Hurricane weather."

Hoddy picked it up. "Said so on my battery radio. But not today." He then got into his jalopy and went off alone; apparently he stopped first at the locksmith's, for around noon the locksmith arrived.

He went about his business with a will, including the locks on the back door, the door from the little terrace above the tennis court, and the door to the upper terrace; he handed shiny new keys to Meade when he left.

The keys did not give her any greater sense of safety. She almost asked him to change the lock on her bedroom door and then told herself that was

180

nonsense. Besides, by that time he had gone, and Florrie had returned and would answer none of the questions Aunt Chrissy put to her.

The sky seemed steadily to thicken; from the terrace the Sound reflected a kind of impenetrable but curiously threatening gray. It was an eerie light, tinged faintly with yellow, yet every leaf, every patch of shrubbery, every tree took on a remarkable distinctness as if they all had remarkable new lives, or were hushed and waiting for something they knew was on its way.

Early in the afternoon, with Hoddy still away and after a makeshift lunch which Florrie did not deign to prepare and neither Aunt Chrissy nor Meade had any heart to undertake beyond a sandwich or two, Mr. Bacon arrived.

He came swirling up the driveway in a chauffeur-driven car. He did not personify the coming hurricane but his news might as well have. At Meade's invitation he settled himself in the library, nodded when Aunt Chrissy evinced her desire to hear what he had to say, made a tent of his manicured fingers, looked around the library and then met Meade's eyes. "It is not good news, Mrs. Havlock," he said. "I'd like to cushion it for you, but I really don't see how I can. Besides, the radio says a storm is coming and I want to get back to the city before it breaks. The fact is"—he took a quick breath and eyed her fixedly—"the fact is, there is no three hundred million dollars."

Aunt Chrissy gave a stifled little cry. He said quickly, "There may be a little we can save out of it. Enough perhaps, for you, Mrs. Havlock, and your aunt. I can't be sure."

He sighed. Meade leaned back in her chair. She felt a little as if the breath had been knocked out of her, and yet as if somehow, someway she had been restored to herself. Mainly, however, she was only bewildered and Mr. Bacon's bright gray eyes perceived this, for he went on hurriedly, "I finally

181

got hold of his secretary, Miss Bellamy, at Treetops I told you about. It seems you can watch the animals—"

"Please, Mr. Bacon," Aunt Chrissy said sharply.

"Ah yes, yes. We, my colleagues and I, have been busy checking on Mr. Havlock's affairs—yes, yes, very busy, very complicated." He glanced nervously at Aunt Chrissy. "The long and short of it is, he didn't have three hundred million. He told me that was the approximate amount of his fortune when we made out his will. He even gave me some lists of stock and all that. It seems he was"—he paused, eyed his neat fingers and said in a remote way—"mistaken."

"Oh," Meade said.

"Naturally, this is a great disappointment to you," he went on rapidly. "But you had to know sometime and I thought it better—"

Aunt Chrissy pulled herself together. "What do you mean?"

"Just that. Miss Bellamy appears to have been in his confidence. She was deeply grieved to know of his death. But she could tell us a number of facts, yes—"

"What facts?" Aunt Chrissy cut through his hesitation.

He went on rapidly again, "To put it briefly, then, he simply spent money as if it were water. He has been giving too lavishly, to all sorts of civic or charitable causes. He bought anything at all he took a fancy to. He seems to have paid no attention to the state of his own finances. Miss Bellamy told us that she knew what he was doing, but naturally—yes, quite naturally—saw no way to remonstrate with him. I daresay," he interpolated reflectively, "that Miss Bellamy's own finances have not suffered. No. It is my considered opinion that she may have profited considerably by Mr.

182

Havlock's spending—really most inconsiderate and improvident spending."

"Do you mean that Miss Bellamy—" Aunt Chrissy began, but Mr. Bacon was horrified.

"Oh no, no! I implied nothing of the kind. I am sure that her relations with Mr. Havlock were merely those of a devoted employee to her employer. Nothing else. I beg you not to suggest an—a—an illicit romance!"

"Afraid, huh?" Aunt Chrissy muttered as if to herself. "Don't want to engage in slander, huh?"

"I am only speaking the truth," Mr. Bacon all but snapped at her. "The plain fact is that he bought too much, gave too much, gave everywhere. I really don't know why. But he took out mortgages, he sold Emmeline stock (it has gone down, by the way, very remarkably, since his death). He—why, even this house is mortgaged to the hilt. I daresay it will have to be sold. As for the apartment in New York, that was taken for mortgages this spring as soon as you came out here for the summer. Yacht, too. In fact, everything we could trace is either mortgaged, taken over by the mortgagee, or sold. Apparently, however, he had been doing this for some years, even before his marriage, Mrs. Havlock. It is only recently that he managed to get down to the bare bones of not only his resources but his credit. You had no idea of this?"

Meade shook her head.

Mr. Bacon said, rapidly, again, with a kind of relief as if he had gotten over the most difficult part of his errand, "Now we'll see to it that you have all the figures and reports, naturally. As I say, I fancy we may be able to salvage something. How much remains to be seen. I must go."

He jumped up, looking visibly relieved. "The radio says the hurricane is coming much sooner than was expected. I took a chance, indeed, coming out here to see you. We may be cut off. However, I felt that you must know and it was my duty—yes, yes, my duty—" He was holding out a dry hand to Meade. She took it; he gave a quick bow in Aunt Chrissy's direction and all but ran toward the door. Meade followed him absently, arriving at the front door to see him skipping down the steps to the long black limousine. The chauffeur was already at the car's door and looked, and probably was, scared of the ominous sky and the strange hot small breeze sifting through the trees. The limousine whirled down the driveway and disappeared.

Meade stood for a moment thinking, trying to reconcile the true state of Sam's finances with his recklessly generous acts. It was not possible!

Aunt Chrissy said behind her. "So that's that. I wouldn't have thought it of Sam."

"Mr. Bacon said he thought there'd be enough for both of us." Meade intended it to be a comfort, but that was not necessary.

Aunt Chrissy was not only resiliant, she was also philosophical. "We are no worse off than when you married Sam. Probably better. But, we have not heard the last of all this. I feel sure that when a full report is made to you, there'll be"—oh yes, she was indomitable—"more money than he thinks now. Of course, Sam may have been giving this Miss Bellamy quite a sum. And possibly"—her eyebrows lifted—"just possibly, this Mr. Bacon has lined his own pockets."

"Oh no!"

"It has been known to happen," Aunt Chrissy said dryly. "And if so, then he or possibly she had a motive for getting rid of Sam. Facts, he said. That's an outstanding fact. Who would have a better opportunity to know how to get his clean"—she snorted and repeated—"clean hands on Sam's fortune. Oh yes..."

"But, Aunt Chrissy, Miss Bellamy was in Kenya. Mr. Bacon wasn't even here when Sam—"
184

"How do we know?" Aunt Chrissy fixed her with an eaglelike gaze. "How do we know either of them couldn't have employed John or somebody to put that poison in Sam's drink? No, mark my words, Meade, this story takes some proving!"

"I think he's telling the truth."

"Then why on earth would Sam waste all that money?"

"Perhaps he didn't have so much in the first place," Meade said slowly.

"Why would he tell Bacon that he did have three hundred million?"

"Oh, I don't know! But honestly, Aunt Chrissy, I can't really feel sorry. I mean for my own sake. It would have been an awful burden..."

"Nonsense," Aunt Chrissy said firmly. Another hot little breeze swept in through the door. She closed it hard. "Right now," she said with her usual emphasis, "I really think the hurricane is coming nearer. I feel it."

So do I, Meade thought. It was as if some force were bearing down upon them.

"Get that little battery radio of Hoddy's, Meade."

Meade did not pause to pick up the oddments of clothing, tennis gear, a strange melee of socks and shirts which were strewn on the floor of Hoddy's room. The radio was under his pillow and still going; she hoped the battery would last, for the first words she heard were: "...strengthening as it approaches the shoreline...evacuation of Fire Island...evacuation of all coastal areas...The Red Cross number...The Coast Guard..."

The radio was skipping a few lines here and there, or rather the words were interspersed unintelligibly, probably by other television news and other radio broadcasts. She carried the radio down to the library.

"Well," Aunt Chrissy said, after listening. "Of course we almost always have hurricanes in

September. There were two others, remember, neither one amounted to anything but a lot of storm warnings. Both went right straight out to sea, but this one..." She held the radio closer and turned shocked eyes and a red face to Meade. "*Meade!* Did you hear that? They've named this one Chrissy!"

"Oh no!" Meade couldn't have checked a hysterical giggle. "Oh no, Aunt Chrissy!"

Aunt Chrissy's face resumed a more normal color; she said with dignity, "It's a perfectly good name!"

"They've got to name them something," Meade said consolingly, although Aunt Chrissy seemed more pleased now than insulted.

Florrie teetered in, on her high heels; she was carrying another battery radio, and amid its squalling storm warnings, her voice rose shrilly. "What did Sam do with all that money? Why?"

She didn't bother now to say Mr. Havlock. Aunt Chrissy said, "You were listening."

Florrie turned a furious glare upon her. "Why not? I have a right. But I can't see why he did this."

Meade said wearily, "I don't know anything about it, Florrie. Only what Mr. Bacon told me."

Florrie eyed her. The radio gave a monotonous warning: "...all coastal areas be prepared for high tides..." Florrie said, "I want to leave. I've got no money. I used up every cent I had on the taxi this morning. I want to get out of here right now."

"I don't have much," Meade said. "I'll see—"

"Don't give her any," Aunt Chrissy said, but Meade remembered leaving her handbag on a bench in the hall and went to it. She had carried it to church the day of the services. In it there was still the message typed by Mrs. Dunham when it couldn't have been typed by Mrs. Dunham because she was then— Meade wouldn't let herself think of the sodden mass the boys had pulled out of the Sound.

186

There was no money in the bag. Naturally, having been accessible to Hoddy! She went upstairs to her room, where as a rule she kept a little roll of bills in a drawer of the chest.

The bills were still there.

A suicide note was there also.

At first she merely looked at the folded paper; then she opened it. It was headed *Havlock Place*. It was a sheet of the fine writing paper Sam always ordered and kept in stock. She didn't immediately understand the words; then she understood too well. The note read:

I killed him. I didn't think the stuff I took from the vet would work just like that and so fast but I—oh, I don't know why I did it. I had to. Sam couldn't taste it. He had no sense of taste. I put it in his drink. I wish now that I hadn't. I'll always wish—I've got to take this way out, the same

It ended there.

It was typewritten but jaggedly, as if in bursts.

It meant that someone intended it to convince the police, convince everyone that she—Meade—had purposely killed Sam. And was going to kill herself.

"Oh no!" She thrust the sheet of paper away from her and yet was horribly aware of every word, every letter.

The wind rattled the vines outside the windows. Wisteria, climbing there, trembled.

Whoever wrote the note—well, who did write it? On house stationery! Someone free to come and go in the house, that was clear. Someone had crept into her room and left an empty bottle in the same drawer—at the same time? Never mind all that, she told herself. Just give it to the police. Tell them how I found it. Tell them—

Yes, tell them. But not now, for an onslaught of wind almost shook the house. She shoved the letter in the pocket of her slacks for safety's sake, to show everybody, to show Andy—but not now. The hurricane was too near. It was really upon them. She was cold and numb with shock—and afraid.

She ran for the stairs; Aunt Chrissy, even Florrie, seemed to promise safety. Florrie couldn't have written that note. Meade thought, wildly; nobody could have written it but there it was, written in advance of—face it, in advance of her own murder and to explain it. The empty bottle was to have been proof.

No, no, no! The tap of her flying feet on the stairs, along the hall, seemed to repeat it: "No, no, no!"

Hoddy came dashing through the front door and flung himself against it. "It's coming," he cried. "How about the windows?"

"You mean boarding them up?" Her voice seemed false, high, unreal. "I don't think we've ever boarded up windows."

"Probably you've never had a real bad hurricane here," Aunt Chrissy said, coming in from the library. "Now, if you'd been in the 1938 hurricane, as I was—"

"I couldn't have been," Hoddy shouted and made for the stairs going down to the driveway again.

"Now where is he going?"

With an immense effort Meade replied, "I've no idea. Aunt Chrissy, I don't know anything we *can* do."

"We are terribly exposed here of course, but high. That's an advantage. We'll not be flooded out."

The telephone rang. Again as if lifting a heavy load, Meade answered. It was Agnes. "Miss Chrissy—oh, it's you, Meade. Brice didn't want me to go with him today. We turned on the radio after we left your place last night and heard about the storm coming. So he told me to stay with you. Our house is so close to the water..."

Agnes promised safety too! "Do come, Agnes. But hurry!"

The gusts of wind dropped into utter, breathless quiet. It, too, had an ominous quality as if something, somewhere, but something bad, were merely holding its breath.

"It's always like this in a hurricane," Aunt Chrissy said. "Really seems as if there is something way out there somewhere just waiting to pounce down and catch us. You watch the birds. Even the birds are nervous, hopping and zooming around this way and that. I'm surprised the dogs haven't made a sound."

The dogs! Their kennels were much lower than the house. Meade ran down the steps and Aunt Chrissy cried, "You can't bring those creatures in the house."

"It's my house!" Meade shouted back.

Florrie materialized behind Aunt Chrissy. "You're not sure of that," she shrieked into the heavy, ominous silence. "Did you bring me some money?"

It was simpler not to reply. Meade ran on through the waiting stillness. If someone intended to murder her—murder her?—this would be a chance. She was alone, running down the steps in such a stillness that her footsteps seemed very loud, betraying her presence, offering her as a target. Nothing anywhere moved.

She reached the kennel fence and nobody sat on the bench waiting for her as Mrs. Dunham had waited. Was it really Mrs. Dunham, or was it someone disguised as Mrs. Dunham? Wildly her surmise shot to the elusive Miss Bellamy. Miss Bellamy could have known just how to approach Sam, just how to accomplish everything that had been accomplished. Miss Bellamy wouldn't have killed Sam. Or would she? In a long and close relationship there might have existed reason for

189

that murder. Yet surely if Mrs. Dunham had in fact been Miss Bellamy, she must have given herself away. Besides, Sam would have known all about such a masquerade and connived at it. But then—oh no, that couldn't have been, for Mrs. Dunham had been murdered herself and Miss Bellamy was on safari. They had been able to reach her by telephone. Mrs. Dunham could never be talked to again.

No, Mrs. Dunham had not been Miss Bellamy.

Yet Aunt Chrissy had a swift mind. Miss Bellamy had certainly known of Sam's perilous financial state. Perhaps that was why she had got herself, at least temporarily, out from under, so to speak, out from under the collapse she must have seen coming.

Meade's hands brushed back leaves of shrubbery. Even the leaves felt hot and strangely quiescent.

Mr. Bacon? Yes, either he or Miss Bellamy might possibly have engineered Sam's murder (and Mrs. Dunham's murder, too) by employing John. John or Florrie.

It had been known to happen. An attorney of standing and supposed integrity, somehow making away with his client's property. It had happened.

But what about the bottle and the clear and terrifying suicide note?

The dogs had their noses at the gate of the kennel fence. Their tails wagged furiously as she approached but even the dogs were too quiet. She opened the gate. Marcelline nudged up to her swiftly; the other two crowded close to her knees. They're scared too, she thought. But only afraid of a coming storm, not of a suicide note.

They followed her, leaping to be as close as they could. No one came out of the trees or shrubbery; no one came up the steps behind her. They reached the front door, with its shining, new lock. In the hall, Aunt Chrissy said, "Now, if Hoddy were here, he'd say, 'What a night for murder.'"

Meade stopped in her tracks; the dogs pushed and muttered. "What do you mean by that?"

"Nothing, I hope. It's only that—well, the night Sam was murdered, Hoddy sat there on the balustrade and said, 'What a night for murder,' something like that. I didn't pay any attention to it. But Hoddy—however, I really don't think he'd murder Sam, no matter how much he wanted money."

Fourteen

After a while it seemed to Meade that her heart began to beat again. She turned steadily, really, to close the screen door. The three dogs stood in the hall together and looked at her. As a rule, when let into the house, they ran, leaping, sniffing, exploring and always winding up in the kitchen.

Finally Meade recovered the use of her voice. *"Hoddy did not kill Sam."*

"I just said I didn't think so," Aunt Chrissy said, looking over Meade's shoulder and added, "Here comes Agnes."

She was in one of the Garnets' two cars, the good one, kept shining and in good repair and not left to the mercies of young Pete, barely fourteen and not really permitted to drive, but who, yet, somehow managed to drive. She wondered absently how many fines his father had paid or if young Pete had contrived to get a learner's permit. Agnes slid out, her lovely slim legs agile, her hand with Sam's great emerald clutching a small airplane bag. "I brought a toothbrush and not much else," she said but with a rather high-pitched and unnatural laugh.

Hoddy came up the drive after her, and no doubt thrilled at the thought of being at the wheel of so beautiful a car, offered to drive it to the garage—another of the few changes Sam had permitted about the house, for it was big, solid and thoroughly modern, even supplied a gas pump.

Meade thought vaguely again of Hoddy's probable reaction when he learned that there was no three hundred million. It did not matter. Nothing really mattered except the threat of a suicide note to be found after Meade's own death. Oh no! she told herself, and then, But be careful. Watch. Don't take chances. It would be some innocent-appearing murder. Why, of course! It could be more of the drug Waldo had had. The empty bottle was put in her room to frame her, and also to prove that she had killed herself!

She couldn't reason logically; she only knew the threat for what it was. A part of her consciousness took in faces and people around her and what they were saying and doing.

Aunt Chrissy had heard something on the radio in her hand; now she held it to her ear. "If Brice is going east along the coast, he had better change his mind and hit for an inland town. Just listen to this."

It was hard to make out anything sensible; too many stations were having too much to say—that, or Hoddy's radio was as battered as most of Hoddy's possessions contrived to be. He came running up the steps and into the wide hall. He handed Agnes the ignition key. "That's a great car!"

"Where have you been?" Aunt Chrissy asked.

194

"Talking to Andy. He borrowed my car."

Meade heard that. "Andy! When a hurricane is coming! Where is he going? What's he trying to do?"

"Lord, I don't know. He just asked for the keys and took off. Didn't even say could he have it or thank you. Seemed to be in a hurry."

The wind was rising—a mere shriek out of all that stillness, but it sounded like an alarm. There was something about the architecture of the big living room, built high above the water, which, when the wind blew suddenly and sharply as it did then, made it sound like the shriek of someone in torment. Everybody jumped; Meade, even though she knew where the shriek came from and why, felt the tiny hairs stir on the back of her neck. After crouching threateningly, Marcelline rose, fixed her eyes in the direction of the living room and growled. Her sons took their cue from her and growled too. Hoddy said nervously, "What are they going to do?" and edged toward the stairs.

"Nothing. There's something about the windows in the living room that shrieks like that," Meade told him. Her voice didn't sound like her own. She wasn't even sure she had spoken.

Aunt Chrissy gave a rather grim laugh. "Sounds like that shriek somebody arranged in the cabin of—you know, in *Uncle Tom's Cabin*... what's his name—Legree! That's it. Legree. A slave had a bottle fixed in the window so it shrieked, and everybody—"

"Darling," Agnes said with a rather tense and unnatural smile, "you're giving away your age!"

"As if you hadn't read the book yourself!" Aunt Chrissy said. "Anyway, the wind is quiet now."

Hoddy leaned more nonchalantly against the newel post, but his ears seemed to twitch nervously. The dogs arranged themselves around Meade's feet but also kept their ears alert.

The stillness, the utter breathless silence had

returned after that one warning shriek. But suddenly a car came hurtling up the drive. The dogs ran to the door as Haggerty loomed up beyond the screen door. Meade let him in. He looked very tired. "I know it's going to storm but I think there's time. I have a little evidence, but not much. I only want to see if any of you"—his weary eyes went around the circle; Meade wasn't sure that he didn't include the intent gaze of the three dogs, who apparently had decided instinctively that this was nobody to bite or even growl at—"knew about it."

He sat down, and Meade, in her strangely faraway voice, suggested iced tea. Hoddy had better sense and mixed him a whiskey.

"About what?" Aunt Chrissy asked. "New evidence?"

"No evidence. Just tag ends of information. Mrs. Garnet"—he looked at Agnes—"did you know that your husband employed a representative of one of the pollsters? I mean, one of the companies who regularly poll opinion."

"Oh yes. But I don't remember much about it. I believe it was just one of what he called bits of political machinery."

Haggerty nodded and drank. "Mr. Havlock did the same?"

Meade shook her head and debated; should she give Haggerty the suicide note now?

Agnes said, "Sam always helped Brice. I expect he employed another polling company. He really did a great deal to promote Brice's whole campaign from the beginning right up to when Sam nominated him. Then of course he went with Brice on—oh, the whole political scene." Yet again it struck Meade that there was something forced and unnatural in Agnes' voice. There was no time to try to analyze that.

Haggerty nodded. "I know. Mr. Havlock put every force he had behind your husband's election." His eyes were tired but all the same, they had a piercing quality. "Do you happen to know if, say, Mr. Havlock expected any particular gain from your husband's election? I mean"—as Agnes' lovely eyes looked oddly, almost purposely, blank, as if no thought of political ambitions on Sam's part had ever occurred to her—"suppose some company Mr. Havlock was associated with, one that was part of his holding company, for instance, wanted to get something that the governor of the state could promote. Like, say, a contract to build a nuclear reactor or an airline terminal. Anything like that?"

But Sam no longer owned the Emmeline Company, Meade thought.

Agnes shook her head. "No. I might not know about it, but I think I would know. Sam—" She hesitated and did not say that Sam had reason to be deeply grateful to Brice. She said instead, "They were old friends. Sam was always very generous."

The chief nodded. "I guess he was one of the most generous men with public needs this state has ever had." He finished his drink. "Oh, by the way, we got hold of a girl in Miss Bellamy's office. Miss Bellamy, she said, was the one who wrote the checks and saw to Sam's personal accounts and all that. Miss Bellamy saw the references Mrs. Dunham gave."

"So then—" Agnes began, and the chief said, "Apparently Miss Bellamy approved the references the day before she left on her two-month vacation abroad."

"Sam's executor—I mean Mr. Bacon—telephoned to her. She's at Treetops—" Meade began, and Aunt Chrissy interrupted sharply, "No need to go into that just now, Meade."

Why not? Meade thought. Nothing matters except this piece of paper in my pocket. She pulled at it, tearing the paper, and the chief went on, "The girl said there were nothing but check stubs made

197

out to cash, which the police assumed could mean checks for Mrs. Dunham or for Sam Havlock's own expenses or anything of the sort. Like most blackmailers, Mrs. Dunham preferred to deal in cash. And oh, by the way, John was on parole. Sentence for forgery, but a light sentence. Got paroled, since it was a first time, and then just disappeared. Didn't report to the parole office—that is, in Marrington. His real name is John Dalaway. Miss Isabel saw it on the list of characters in that old movie, and she thinks Mrs. Dunham's name was Rose Swarther." The wind shrieked again. "But he may be using another name by this time. Florrie probably knows it, maybe not."

"Another point—so far we have not found any scrap of evidence about where Mrs. Dunham kept her money. She's probably had a safe-deposit box under another name, heaven only knows where. If we ever find John, maybe we can get the information out of him. Quite a coincidence, both of them turn up here working for Sam Havlock. But that note that got you off, Meade, the one in her desk. Well, she didn't write it. Mr. Garnet wrote it. He admitted it to me."

"Brice did that!" Meade cried, and without intending it, crumpled the suicide note in her hand.

"Oh yes," Agnes said rapidly. "He told me he was going to get Meade out of this if he had to do anything at all. He said he'd pull a rabbit out of a hat, just wait and see. So then, when the note was found, I guessed Brice had written it on Mrs. Dunham's typewriter and left it there for a policeman or somebody to find. It was easy. You know Mrs. Dunham often left her little office open so prospective employers could wait for her there in case she was delayed. I didn't blame him one bit. Think of our long friendship. Think of all the help Sam was to him in his political struggle. Think how dreadful it would be to see Meade go to trial or

198

to—suppose a jury convicted her! We were both perfectly certain that Meade could not have thought of murdering Sam! So Brice did that."

"But that note in my handbag," Meade said slowly. "That was typed too. It was threatening note! *'You'll know what is best for you.'* It was signed, typewritten too, *'Mrs. Dunham.'* But it had to have been written after Mrs. Dunham's murder. Brice couldn't have typed that." But the other note, the note crumpled in her hand, must have been written at the same time the little bottle had been hidden in her room. Why had she been a source of danger to anybody at that time? She would give it to Haggerty now.

Agnes sat down suddenly as if her knees had given way. "Another note?" she whispered.

"We'll have to trace that one," the chief said. "Very simple if we can find the typewriter." He thought for a second. "Start, say, with Mrs. Dunham's typewriter." He turned to Meade. "You might have told me this, you know."

"Yes," Meade replied unhappily. "But, you see, it was so—so—"

"Unimportant," Aunt Chrissy said haughtily.

The chief looked at her. "I don't think I'd say that. Let me see—"

Marcelline gave a sharp, warning yelp and ran for the door. Hoddy followed, beating her by a hair's-breadth and unfortunately stepping on a paw of one of her offspring, who did not help anything by grabbing Hoddy by the ankle. Hoddy howled, Marcelline howled, the wind howled as if getting a second breath, and through it came the rattle of a taxicab going very fast down the driveway. "But I saw her!" Hoddy cried, jumping on one foot and trying to keep the other out of biting range. "I saw her! It was Florrie and she was all dressed up and carried a suitcase."

Without a word the chief ran to the telephone in the pantry. He seemed by now to know his way about the house. Hoddy said he'd get hydrophobia. The chief came out. "Somebody will pick her up if she's trying to get the train to New York. But there's no telling . . . The state police will be alerted, but that's not a sure thing, for she can change taxis, take a bus, get on a train at another station, anything."

"She's running away! She murdered Sam because she thought she'd get some of his money!"

"Of course Mrs. Dunham saw it and black-mailed her and—" Hoddy began.

"She went to the city to get a good firm of lawyers," Meade interrupted. "And I must say I can't blame her. If she thinks, as she does think, that some of Sam's money ought to have gone to her—yes, she's gone for a lawyer. But it seems there's no money." She might as well not have said it. No one paid it or her the least attention. Perhaps she hadn't said it out loud, she thought wildly. No, it was more likely that the rising deafening gusts of wind had drowned her own words. Only Aunt Chrissy understood and gave her a sharp look.

Chief Haggerty didn't listen. He was already at the door. "It seems a long time to wait, Meade, but really, we've had police all over the tristate area working on this. Who was John? Who was Mrs. Dunham? Social Security people, Internal Revenue people. Where is John? We have threads out almost everywhere. We've had men in the city trekking around all the theater agencies, especially those which put together summer stock. It may seem slow to you, but a great deal has been done."

"With no results so far," Aunt Chrissy said.

The chief opened the door, bracing it and himself against the wind. "Miss Isabel helped about that. Seeing them in an old movie under other names. It all takes time, but nobody can disappear forever, not these days, when everything you do or write or say, practically, has a

200

number. I can only say that we—and I mean a great many people—are doing our best to get a line on John's and on Mrs. Dunham's past. Now I've got to hurry—"

He paused though, and listened to Agnes, who linked her hands together, the big emerald shining with green and somehow threatening lights as she said, "I've thought about this ever since I knew about Florrie and Sam. Sam might simply have felt sorry for her and offered her and John a job just because of that. But he might have been amused at revenging himself on a girl who had played such a trick about his marriage."

"Oh no! Not Sam!" But, yes, Meade thought coldly, Sam *could* have done just that. She remembered the barely concealed impertinence with which Florrie had taken any orders from her. "Or," she said suddenly, "she may have accepted it because she thought she could get Sam back."

Agnes looked steadily at her tensely clasped hands. Hoddy said, "Oh, for Lord's sake, Meade! Would Sam have wanted to show off a woman like that as his wife?"

"But, you see," Meade said, "she didn't think of herself as 'a woman like that.' She's vain; she pays a lot of attention to her clothes when she feels like it. Yes, she may have thought she could get Sam back. But she may also have had a notion that there was some way she could still get money out of him."

Hoddy looked scared. "But you get the dough. No question of it."

There's no dough to get, certainly no three hundred million dollars. Far from it. She would tell Hoddy later. It's not important now, Meade thought vaguely. The wind shrieked through the hall like a lost soul and also as if it might threaten them, knowing that there were immediate dangers in the air and coming nearer at every breath.

The chief cried, "I've got to hurry. This will

mean the phone lines are down. Electric lines. Do you have plenty of battery flashlights?"

Hoddy, of course, knew. "Eleven. I was prowling around—I mean, wandering around one day—"

"'Prowling' is the *mot juste*," Aunt Chrissy said acidly.

"Anyway, I counted them. I'll get them together now and fasten down the terrace furniture, too, in case."

Agnes shot up like a spring suddenly released. "I've got to go home! Good heavens, I left the notes for Brice's speech tomorrow night on the terrace. There's time before the storm strikes if I hurry."

Agnes followed Hoddy out the door and they clattered down the steps. The chief had already disappeared, thudding heavily down the steps, and the crumpled suicide note was still in Meade's pocket. Yet what could he, what could anyone do just then in all the wicked hurly-burly of a hurricane? As soon as it had gone, she would find the chief.

Aunt Chrissy said thoughtfully, "I keep thinking that Sam must have kept records somewhere. Seems odd that none of Sam's forebears, or Sam himself for that matter, ever had a safe built in the house."

Again there was a kind of tinkle way back in Meade's memory; it was something very small, barely a flicker of recognition. But there must have been something of a joke about it; she could almost see Sam's face, smiling, his white teeth glimmering in some kind of rather dark room.

The house was dark and empty except for the dogs. The wind steadily and heavily continued.

"Gusts up to ninety miles or more," the radio said.

Aunt Chrissy sighed. "Personal records, I mean. Things he wouldn't have in his office. This Miss Bellamy might not have known everything—"

Then she knew! "Aunt Chrissy! He did leave

202

personal records! Or something. Right here in the house!"

"But the police searched ..."

"Only in his desk. They didn't know about this. It's not a safe. It's downstairs in the cellars, where Hoddy always said pirates could find useful hiding places. It wasn't of course a pirate hiding place. But Sam told me. The first time we came here, after our honeymoon, he was showing me all around the house, even the ground floor—the cellars below. He laughed and pointed toward it. He said it was an antiquated old thing. Nobody was ever likely to look at it. And it held only some"—Meade caught her breath—"some personal records. Don't you see?"

Aunt Chrissy looked at her steadily for a moment, then she went to the hall bar, took a glass and poured a generous measure of her special drink in it. She brought it to Meade and said, surprisingly for Aunt Chrissy, "Down the hatch with this! Then go and look."

The drink stung her throat, so that she couldn't speak for a moment but only wave her hands and cough and push Marcelline off her knee. Aunt Chrissy apparently took this for an injunction to feed the dogs, two of whom, with the unfailing interest of a dog for a kitchen, were shoving at the pantry door with impatient little barks and whimpers.

"I'll feed them," Aunt Chrissy said, "while you look at this ... this place for personal records!"

She swept into the pantry; the dogs hurtled after her, and Meade put down the glass of Southern Comfort and ran for the door under the stairs which led to the cellars. Actually the whole unused ground floor was part cellar and storerooms, and part servants' quarters. These bedrooms were on the side of the house directly above the Sound, so the rather dusty windows did give some light. The other side of the whole floor was entirely composed of furnace, wine racks, and storerooms, most of them probably unentered for years and certainly unused. Usually if a cold spell arrived while they were still summering at the house, wood was brought to the vast fireplaces. She could not remember whether the furnace, looming out of one of the shadowy rooms, had ever, during her marriage, been used. Most of these doors were closed and in the storeroom at the very end of the hall was the hiding place Sam had, laughing as if at some private joke, shown her.

There were dim lights along the narrow hall between former servants' quarters and storerooms. She found a wall switch, which gave a loud click and turned on several bulbs. Servants must have had either rather bad times or unbelievably mild and sweet natures to put up with such accommodations, but then, it had been years and years since those rooms had been in use. The end storeroom was on the right.

In this part of the cellars there were no windows, since it was on the side where the ground had been filled in for the tennis court. The walls were simply blackish concrete. She already felt grimy by the time she reached the end of the hall and the right hand storeroom; the door was closed. She opened it and groped into musty darkness for a switch. Rather to her surprise she found it, and a dim light bulb sprang into being, dangling from a cord in the ceiling. It revealed the hiding place.

It also explained why, despite the fact that the police had searched the house, they had not discovered anything of interest. A vast iron cooking stove stood against the wall; the elaborate nickel trimmings winked slyly at her. It had two enormous cooking ovens and a kind of vat at one side to be kept full of water, heated presumably by the coal fires in the stove; even the pot lids still had a certain glimmer under the dim light of that one ceiling bulb, as if once they had been frequently and proudly polished. She wondered how long the stove had been there. No one could have sold it, not even as an antique, not that monster. Yet she had learned that almost nothing, ever, was thrown away in that house. It might be banished; probably there were ancient refrigerators in other rooms, and trunks—certainly trunks—all of it comprising the accumulation of years.

There were six stove lids, but she could almost see Sam's handsomely manicured hand reaching out for a kind of handle. She put her own hand on the shining nickel of the reservoir for water. She lifted it. The light was too dim for her to see much inside the enameled interior, yet it was still clean and white. And—yes, there was a bundle of papers, tied with brown string. Shrinking, certain that somehow spiders might have crept into this safe hiding place, she groped further and pulled it out.

She hadn't heard anything or anybody. She was standing under the one dim bulb, clutching the papers in one hand and holding the stove lid in the other when Agnes said, "What on earth are you doing?" She stood staring at Meade under the dim light.

"Agnes! Oh, you scared me."

"I came back. The storm is getting so bad I was afraid to go on home." Marcelline was there too, standing very still and square.

"Oh dear, Brice's speech. Agnes, this old stove! Sam showed it to me and laughed and he said he had some personal things in it. In there, where water was heated. He never mentioned it again. I remembered just now and found this! Papers of some kind."

"Give them to Brice. He's the one to see to them. Oh, here, is this your drink? Smells like Aunt Chrissy's. I saw it in the hall." She had the glass in her hand. "Didn't you hear me call you?"

"How can anybody hear anything in a storm like this? Thank you, Agnes. Let's get out of this place. I feel as if spiders are walking around!"

"Sure. Here, take this." She put her glass in Meade's hand.

Marcelline stood very straight behind her. Agnes laughed. "I saw the open cellar door and Marcelline coming down, so I knew you were here. Finish your drink, it's spilling. Sam must have been very amused about using this old thing for a hiding place." She took Meade's arm and started for the door. Marcelline made a kind of subterranean grumble. Meade drank some of the liquor, mainly owing to some innate housekeeping instinct reminding her that all that sticky liquor would be impossible to clean up, and then, startled as its fiery sting, said, "Don't pull my wrist so hard, Agnes. Wait a minute, I'll put this drink—" She paused. It certainly had a peculiar taste!

Agnes said, pulling her arm with amazing strength for such a slender woman, "I don't blame you for not liking it. Sam didn't taste it. He had no sense of taste. You knew that. I knew it. But he kept it a secret. He was embarrassed about it. But it used to make him laugh to see how people looked and to hear what they said when he drank off that ghastly mixture you always made for him. Sorry, did I hurt you? Go on, finish your drink and we'll get upstairs out of this dusty place."

Meade clutched the papers to her chest, and the suicide note in her slacks pocket crackled. The drink she had tasted did have a peculiar—it had a deadly taste! And she had swallowed...how much? She was screaming. No, she wasn't screaming. That was the wind. Nothing could scream; she couldn't scream; she couldn't move. She could do nothing at all. She was dimly aware of a bewildering, stunning roar of sounds, a mixture of dogs growling and barking, of men's voices, certainly somebody was swearing, and Marcelline howled with fury, and the melee of voices grew louder, but Meade couldn't distinguish anything;

just all at once, as if she were too tired even to hear or stand or move her mouth, and in the rage of sound and thuds and yells and then just nothing at all, she went down and down and down, crumpled against the old stove, yet she couldn't even wriggle her arms or legs to get up, and the waves of the Sound broke and tore at the house as if they meant to demolish the house and her.

Fifteen

A light was blazing down upon her face; she opened her eyes and shut them again quickly to shut out the glare.

Somebody said something; somebody said something else. The wind roared around the house, and the rain now had come with it, slashing at the windows as if determined to break down this thing of cement and wood that defied it. She knew dimly that she was in the big living room on a sofa.

"No use," somebody—Andy?—said. "Make her throw it all up. Here, drink it, Meade. I say, drink—"

"Let me.... I know how.... Give me the glass." What an odd squeaky voice! It said firmly, "Swallow. Hurry, it'll soon come up. Hoddy, get something..."

It tasted awful and it came up. "I hope I didn't

give her too much," said the squeaky voice. "It was mustard and water, but I also used an emetic I use for the dogs— Look out, here's more..."

Somebody was holding her head over an ice bucket. Her whole body shook and strained, and how could she possibly have swallowed so much liquid! She leaned back, and the whole process was instantly repeated until, at last, the squeaky voice said, "I think I got it all up." A strong hand came down on her wrist.

"Oh, she's better," said the squeaky voice and added proudly, "I don't think a real doctor could have done any better. Can you sit up now, Mrs. Havlock?"

Waldo, of course, giving her a treatment he gave sick dogs. It had worked. She was exhausted, trembling, hot and cold and free of that ghastly, stinging nausea.

Andy leaned so close she could feel his face against her own. "My darling. It's all right now. Waldo says so. He got it out of you."

She said weakly, "There's nothing left in me." But actually she couldn't have said it clearly enough for anybody to understand. Waldo's squeaky voice spoke: "Now, get some blankets over her and put some hot-water bottles at her feet. She'll be all right now. But I'll stay right here."

Andy answered, "You get blankets, Aunt Chrissy. Hurry. I can't leave her yet."

"I'm all right," Meade said, but again nobody seemed to hear for Hoddy said, a long way off, "She says she had to do it." Meade said with a great effort, "It was in the drink Agnes brought me. The glass was here in the hall. Anybody could have put that drug in it."

"Not anybody," Andy said. "Agnes."

Of course, yes Agnes. Agnes had held her, Agnes had tried to coax her to drink. She felt again as if all strength had been taken away from her.

210

Andy said, "She tried to frame you, Meade. But clear herself. Her husband defended you, so it wouldn't occur to anybody that his own wife had murdered Sam. But then she couldn't let you live because somebody—you—had to be proved to be Sam's murderer. She wasn't safe until then. It had to be you because you had the opportunity and you were Sam's wife and had a perfect motive. So she picked you to make herself safe forever."

She dug into the pocket of her slacks and handed the crumpled suicide note to Andy. His face hardened as he read it. He handed it to Hoddy, who read and handed it to Waldo. Hoddy said, "She's talking, talking. Now that it's all over, she can't seem to move. I've got her shut in the study. All she keeps saying is that Sam was going to ruin Brice."

Andy said, "Agnes claims she killed Sam to save Brice and her family."

"To save Brice?"

Andy took her hand. "It seems to have happened this way. Agnes says that she and Sam stopped in Waldo's place the day you took Marcelline there. They stopped to pick you up. Waldo wasn't there, so they took a look around the place. Agnes says she saw Sam pick up a half-empty bottle. Sam read the label and said he wondered what 3-dash numbers meant but it must be poison because it was marked with a red skull and crossbones. While Sam was looking for you, Agnes snatched up the bottle and another one just like it from the open cabinet in the room where Waldo keeps his medicines. She says she thought they might come in handy later if Sam persisted in his scheme against Brice."

Hoddy broke in, "She knew all about that horrible cocktail Sam used to drink."

Meade was dizzily yet firmly taking hold of her reason. "Agnes and Brice knew that Sam had no sense of taste. I knew it. Nobody else. So—"

Hoddy broke in excitedly, "Agnes dropped the poison in Sam's drink and Sam couldn't tell what it tasted like."

The storm howled and surged and pushed, a living determined force, at all the windows. Aunt Chrissy came hurrying in, half hidden with blankets which she piled on top of Meade, covering even her face.

Meade fought off the fleecy blankets. "Tell me everything."

"We can't tell you everything," Andy replied. "But we can tell you most of it. Some is conjecture."

"Tell me," Meade said again.

Much of it had to be speculation, but the papers Meade had found in the old stove were evidence. Brice, very poor then, finishing his law course, had quietly stolen a large sum of money from Sam, who carelessly left large amounts of cash anyplace where he happened to put it. Sam had discovered the theft. Brice was his only friend (he didn't make friends easily, even then), but he made Brice sign a confession, told him Brice could repay him some-time and then let the matter drop. Back in his mind, though, there may have been a secret notion that something might render this confession of some use to him. Sam must have been, always, a very complex character. Meantime, all through the years, they had apparently been the best of friends. Brice, indeed, seemed to have completely believed in Sam until...

Even knowing, as he must have known, how little money he had left, Sam gave largely everywhere until he was exceedingly popular in the state; he nominated Brice for governor; he went with him constantly to political meetings. He made himself so important a part of the picture of Brice as governor that he would almost certainly be the choice of the party for the governor's seat—if he could get rid of Brice.

212

When Andy, who turned out to be the one who'd taken the time and trouble, had the infinite patience to seek out and interview party members, he discovered that both Brice and Sam had paid for confidential polls of public opinion. The result of each poll was that without Brice, Sam would have been the overwhelming choice for governor.

"And Sam might have schemed to recoup some of the money he had thrown around so recklessly. Elected officials have been known to get their hands on money," Aunt Chrissy said dourly.

Brice had confided to Agnes that lately Sam had been hinting to him, jokingly at first, then more and more seriously, how upset the voters would be if they learned, accidentally of course—through little hints to the press that might start rumors—that their candidate for governor had helped himself to a substantial sum of money years ago—and from his best friend, too, the state's most popular and benevolent citizen. Brice told Agnes that he was even considering withdrawing from the governorship race. He'd dream up some excuse about ill health or family problems. Agnes suddenly saw all her dreams for the future disappearing before her very eyes—the justification for her faith and love for Brice—for having chosen him instead of Sam and his money years ago.

When Agnes saw Sam inspecting the bottle of poison, she must have felt a wave of presentiment. She knew instinctively that it might be useful later. When Sam had gone out to the street looking for Meade, who was then sitting in the drugstore drinking a malted milk—she now remembered and could not believe that such an ugly drama was going on so quietly near her—Agnes had gone quickly through Waldo's backroom stores of medicine. (At this point Waldo rubbed his hair uneasily and said he couldn't be expected to keep order in his office; he had too much to do.) Agnes must have found in the same box from the supplier another bottle resembling the one she already had, and quietly and swiftly had taken it too.

The real, hard-working campaign was very near; she'd have to get rid of Brice's unwelcome, but not yet declared opponent—who would be declared as soon as Sam decided the time was ripe to persuade Brice, blackmail him really, into withdrawing from the election. She had wept over and over, Andy said soberly, that she hadn't a doubt as to its being a truly lethal poison, but she didn't know how it would affect Sam; there was a danger there; there was no danger in quietly slipping the contents into Sam's well-known cocktail, there on the table. She thought she had accomplished it without being seen, but when she looked behind her, Mrs. Dunham's black dress had rustled swiftly out of sight. And then—then it happened. Not at all as Agnes had expected it to happen, but even more fortunately from her point of view; it had been a daring feat; there was no way for her to guess even what Sam's reaction might be; she had never expected that quiet, instant collapse. She had run down with the others pretending to try to help Sam.

Agnes and Brice had known of Sam's hiding place in the old stove. She refused to admit this so far, but Andy said she must have known of it. Sam had told them, probably. After all, they were his oldest and best friends—the only ones he really had. She had come to the house, after being turned back by the storm. The house seemed empty. A glass of Aunt Chrissy's drink stood on the table near the stairs—the door to the cellars was open and Marcelline was starting down. So, she reasoned, Meade must be in the cellars. She must know about the stove. Nobody so far had mentioned it. Even Brice did not know exactly where it was. Marcelline was certainly following Meade. Agnes still had the second bottle she had taken;

she poured its contents into the glass and went down the stairs and found Meade, stove door open, hands and face grimy and in her hands a package of papers, tied with cord, which Agnes guessed accurately told of Brice's long-ago theft. So she had acted promptly, swiftly, instinctively.

Andy had never felt entirely satisfied with the accuracy of Waldo's memory and certainly not with the untidy and hurried manner in which Waldo nevertheless managed to conduct a successful but too busy career. So that afternoon he had pinned down Waldo's memory and searched through the books, where presumably Waldo kept his records; there was at last a record of two remaining bottles numbered 3-dash and labeled "Poison," and both had disappeared. Waldo had known nothing of them since he had given the small dose to Marcelline. "Two bottles," Andy said. "It's simple when you look at it. Agnes took them both, she used one in Sam's drink and then hid the empty bottle"—Andy squeezed Meade's hand hard—"trying to frame you. She had to find a murderer to keep herself and Brice safe. The second bottle was still in Agnes' possession and she tried to make you take it."

So Andy and Waldo had come to the house, and in the driveway they met Hoddy, who had just finished checking the windows and securing the outdoor furniture.

"I see." Aunt Chrissy glanced around her as if for support, found no bottle of her favorite drink and said, as if reciting a lesson, "I see."

Each of them could fill in the gaps, although in fact there were few gaps. There were plenty of ways Agnes could have concealed the empty bottle at the time of the discovery of Sam's body; any place, behind some book, in the cushions of some sofa. She had also had plenty of chances to remove the empty bottle and then—sure that if she framed Meade later, after Brice presumably had rescued

215

her from an indictment for murder, nobody could believe that she or Brice was the murderer; she had slipped back into the house through the lower terrace door, which was seldom if ever locked, and into Meade's room, where she had hidden the bottle.

Even the dogs would not have objected to this; they knew her, but just in case, she had the presence of mind to open their gate and leave the main driveway gate open, so they had hurtled happily down the road to Waldo.

The result of the conference between Waldo and Andy was the clear conclusion that somewhere there was another bottle full of poison, and it had to be somewhere. They came, bucking against the wind and rain. Hoddy joined them at the steps. They, too, had seen the cellar door open as it never was; they had heard a kind of scuffle and murmur of voices and had run down the stairs to find Agnes trying to force the rest of the drink down Meade's throat.

They dragged her away, and all at once Agnes began to cry, great wracking sobs, and the only words she kept saying were, "It was for Brice, it was for Brice."

"So she killed Mrs. Dunham. Blackmailing her, I suppose," Aunt Chrissy said calmly. "And she encouraged Brice to write that letter to protect Meade."

"That," said Andy, rather sadly, "that actually was to protect herself, too. If he got Meade off, then who would think that maybe Brice or Agnes had any motive for the murder. Why, he himself, *intentionally*, had saved Meade! Would he go to such lengths to save a suspected murderer unless he intended to show to the world that he and his wife were not involved, for if they had been, then of course he'd have let Meade take the rap. Oh, she had it all figured out. She didn't want Brice involved in a lengthy trial, he would save Meade

216

quickly—so nobody could possibly suspect him, her lawyer, or his wife, her friend. But if he had any connection with Sam's murder, anybody would think, then he wouldn't have cared who took the blame, even Meade."

Meade suddenly spoke and everybody hushed to listen to her as if she had newly risen from some frightful pit of danger, which as a matter of fact was true. "The suicide note...the empty bottle in my bedroom..."

Andy took a long breath and seemed to force himself to bare facts. "Now then, whoever put that bottle there had to be someone who knew the house, knew the door which was scarcely used, rarely if ever locked—that or somebody in the house, and I didn't think it was Florrie or John—I don't know why, I just didn't. But I did begin to think of the extra vigorous way Sam appeared to boost Brice's political career. He—I can't explain, but somehow I felt that Sam did too much in helping Brice, always present, you know, at Brice's elbow so to speak, making speeches for Brice on his own, too. Yes, I did begin to wonder if Brice saw a dangerous rival in Sam. Agnes has been talking, Meade, talking and—it's horrible. She's hysterical, crying and not making much sense but enough," Andy said grimly. "Oh yes, she wanted to frame you with that bottle merely to be sure that you would be accused and then Brice would be protected when he got you off and showed everybody that he himself must be completely free of suspicion. Later she had to murder Mrs. Dunham, for she must have tried to blackmail her. Probably hated it but had to kill her. Easy, I suppose, in a way, for an athlete like Agnes, coaxing her into her own car, then—but we can surmise all that. I imagine the police will be able to prove that the scarf belonged to Agnes and not Mrs. Dunham. As to Agnes' killing Sam, I expect she could always have said to herself, 'But I didn't know that stuff was so lethal,' or 'I was only trying it, thought it would be a good joke on Sam for drinking that ghastly cocktail'—something like that." He paused and then said soberly, "What you must understand, Meade, is that Agnes' ambition for Brice and herself was always there. It had to be. A driving, completely dedicated ambition for his political career. It had meant more to her than anything. So much that she'd have taken any chance to get what she wanted. So she did. Even to that suicide note—" Andy went to one of the windows. "I think it's letting up. I'll see if the phone is all right."

"It wasn't a few minutes ago," Hoddy said. "I tried it when I was looking for candles."

So that accounted for some of the strangeness of the scene, Meade thought vaguely; there was no electric light; there were candles blazing and wavering everywhere, on the tables, on the mantel, giving the room a hideous gala appearance.

Hoddy said, "I'll try the phone again. And check on Agnes. I probably shouldn't have left her alone."

"Good God," said Andy and ran out of the room.

They shouldn't have left her alone. The study was empty. The front door was open and the wind stormed through the hall, but Agnes had gone.

"I'll report to Haggerty," Hoddy cried and ran for the telephone, which was now usable, for the storm had blown itself out to sea.

"Find Brice, Brice!" Meade said, heartsick—but safe.

Later, Andy took her to see Brice. The storm had left much of its wreck behind it, fallen trees, wires down, the policemen out with flashing red lights, warning any passer-by of live wires. A fireman was climbing up a pole with some strangely covered and shielded instrument in his hand. "He's going to cut that live wire," Andy said. "I wouldn't have his job. And they said we only got the fringe of the hurricane!"

Brice simply took Meade into his arms. Andy left them. But in the end there wasn't much to say. "It was to save you, Brice—you and your career. She really loves you very much," Meade told Brice, trying to comfort him.

But Brice said firmly, "No. A jury won't care about that. No..."

Chief Haggerty himself came in and went to Brice. "I'm sorry, Mr. Garnet. I've bad news. But perhaps it was for the best."

"She's dead," Brice said with certainty.

"You see, this storm raised hell all along the coast. Trees, telephone lines—live wires down. She ran into one—I'm sorry."

Brice's hands held more tightly to Meade's, but his face showed no change. After a moment, though, he said, "It'll be better for the children."

"Sir," said Chief Haggerty. He swallowed hard and said again, "Sir, it may be I can keep much of this story pretty quiet. The storm will be headline news for a week or so, and I'll try. May not be able to do much, but people trust me around here. I can do something."

Brice shook hands with him. Then he turned to Andy. "Take Meade home. I'll be all right. You see, for some time I've begun to feel that Agnes may have had something to do with Sam's death. I showed her some of the pollsters' reports and I knew that she was upset—all her life—her goals. That's why I insisted she send the children away. Then when I told her about Sam's hints—and he died so strangely, so conveniently, I knew. I just knew. It's the kind of devious plan she would think of and— Isn't it ironic, now I'll drop out of the governor's race so Sam will get part of what he wanted after all. Good night, Meade, my dear."

Before he drove away, Chief Haggerty said, "We picked up Florrie at the station. Now that it's all

219

over, she's beginning to talk a bit more. She admitted she's the one who put the television sets out of commission to keep you from seeing John and Mrs. Dunham in the old movie. She thought he was hiding something about their relationship and she had some kind of vague loyal idea of protecting him, and incidentally herself. You two go on home; we'll clear up the details later."

"Brice will be all right, I think. He has his work and the children," Andy said as they picked their way along a street amid fallen branches, telephone lines, such debris as a violent storm leaves behind it.

After negotiating a particularly large clump of branches and an entire maple tree, Andy said, "Now, about your money..."

"Money. Oh, Andy, there isn't any. That is, there may be enough for Aunt Chrissy." She told him quickly as he steered around clumps of fallen trees and tumbled shrubbery. When she had finished he said with a grin, "Hoddy's going to have to go to work."

"Don't you mind?"

"Mind! If I only dared take my hands from this wheel— Look out there, you idiot! Oh, I beg your pardon," he added as a hurried policeman turned a reproachful face on him. "Take your hand off my arm, Meade. I love you, but I've got to get around this tangle of wires."

They managed an uneven course up the driveway, avoiding two heavy branches; the whole place looked as if it had been under shell fire. But Aunt Chrissy met them at the door, strangely jubilant. "That man—that Mr. Bacon got through on the phone. He says the appraisers have opened Sam's big safe-deposit box. And he says—listen to this, Meade—he says all the jewels in it belong to you, no question about that whatever. Even though the money is gone."

Hoddy gave a gasp and a yell. "*What are you*

220

talking about?" Aside from gasping again as if he were under a cold shower, Hoddy really took it very well. He only glanced at Andy and said that it was a good thing Andy would give him a job.

"But you'll have the jewels, Meade," Aunt Chrissy reminded her.

Remembered visions of herself, a kind of make-believe, show-off wife, gave Meade a cold little shiver. "I don't want the jewels, I won't take them!" All the parties, all the places she had worn those jewels to please Sam seemed to whirl dizzyingly through her mind.

"Of course she'll take them," Andy said firmly. "They belong to her and I might need—oh, just a couple of rajah's rubies or a diamond tiara someday when a well doesn't perform."

"You! Why—*why, that's—*" Aunt Chrissy was stuttering. She recovered with smooth aplomb. "I see. No surprise. Isabel and I have decided to share her house. Talked it over. I'll see to the dogs."

ABOUT THE AUTHOR

MIGNON G. EBERHART's name has become a guarantee of excellence in the mystery and suspense field. Her work has been translated into sixteen languages, and has been serialized in many magazines and adapted for radio, television and motion pictures.

For many years, Mrs. Eberhart traveled extensively abroad and in the United States. Now she lives in Greenwich, Connecticut.

In April 1971 the Mystery Writers of America gave Mrs. Eberhart their Grand Master Award, in recognition of her sustained excellence as a suspense writer, and in 1977 she served as president of that organization.

MASTER NOVELISTS

CHESAPEAKE CB 24163 $3.95
by James A. Michener

An enthralling historical saga. It gives the account of different generations and races of American families who struggled, invented, endured and triumphed on Maryland's Chesapeake Bay. It is the first work of fiction in ten years to make its debut as #1 on *The New York Times Best Seller List*.

THE BEST PLACE TO BE PB 04024 $2.50
by Helen Van Slyke

Sheila Callaghan's husband suddenly died, her children are grown, independent and troubled, the men she meets expect an easy kind of woman. Is there a place of comfort? A place for strength against an aching void? A novel for every woman who has ever loved.

ONE FEARFUL YELLOW EYE GB 14146 $1.95
by John D. MacDonald

Dr. Fortner Geis relinquishes $600,000 to someone that no one knows. Who knows his reasons? There is a history of threats which Travis McGee exposes. But why does the full explanation live behind the eerie yellow eye of a mutilated corpse?

8002

GREAT ROMANTIC NOVELS

SISTERS AND STRANGERS PB 04445 $2.50
by Helen Van Slyke

Three women—three sisters each grown into an independent lifestyle—now are three strangers who reunite to find that their intimate feelings and perilous fates are entwined.

THE SUMMER OF THE SPANISH WOMAN
CB 23809 $2.50
by Catherine Gaskin

A young, fervent Irish beauty is alone. The only man she ever loved is lost as is the ancient family estate. She flees to Spain. There she unexpectedly discovers the simmering secrets of her wretched past ... meets the Spanish Woman ... and plots revenge.

THE CURSE OF THE KINGS CB 23284 $1.95
by Victoria Holt

This is Victoria Holt's most exotic novel! It is a story of romance when Judith marries Tybalt, the young archeologist, and they set out to explore the Pharaoh's tombs on their honeymoon. But the tombs are cursed ... two archeologists have already died mysteriously.

8000